The DARK EAGLE

Hope you enjoy

The DARK EAGLE

BETRAYED BY HIS COUNTRY

GREG ZOLLER

Design by Lou Robinson.

Produced and printed in the United States of America

ISBN 978-0-9839768-1-3

Contents

Foreword

Over a decade ago, I was in need of a farrier for my horses and Greg Zoller was highly recommended. Knowing he was a Cornell-trained, highly-respected farrier who had seen the best there is to see in the equine world, I was a bit nervous about him seeing our modest little barn.

Greg arrived on time for our first appointment, as he would every six weeks of the following years. He looked over the first horse—a dominant, intimidating mare—gave her a strong pat, then set about his work quietly and surely, as she gently pushed off his cap and nuzzled him affectionately. His demeanor was that of a competent, gifted professional who didn't need to be pretentious, and I recognized that right away.

Our collection of horses changed over the years and Greg saw my kids drift away from their interest in horses, as I held on to that passion. For a long time, I also held on to a faithful, old, unusable horse because he had been a great friend to many people. As Tare Mr. Solis declined severely in health, Greg continued to care for his hooves as he would a show horse. We talked about what was inevitable and he said I would know when it was time. I never felt judged by Greg on any level, even though he surely must have wondered at times about my sanity.

I looked forward to Greg's visits. He was always thinking about something. Dripping sweat in summer heat and humidity or numb with cold in winter, we talked about family, local news, politics, horses, history and the events he attended to increase his skills.

One day, as he nipped around the edge of the hoof he was holding up and against his leg, Greg said, "I have an idea for a book I'd like to write." I asked, "Oh, what's it about?" He answered, "I believe Benedict Arnold was framed." He offered some details in support of his theory, based on seven or so years of his research.

Greg's announcement really came as no surprise. It felt natural and I didn't doubt for a second that he would follow through if he said he planned to do something. The subject continued to come up over the next several months and I learned he had started a manuscript. As I had worked for some time as a news and history reporter, I offered to look it over, do some editing and type it if he wanted that.

In fall of 2011, Greg arrived one day with three tablets of yellow, legal-sized pages filled with the story he had penned. I was amazed that he had consistently produced that much copy at the end of long days spent with horses around the Finger Lakes region. The work of a farrier is about as demanding, and sometimes dangerous, as any work gets.

To see Greg's book go from handwriting to print has been an enjoyable experience. In the process, I've been reminded of how fascinating and intricate is the history of America, particularly during the Revolution. It's easy to imagine Greg Zoller taking his place on the patriot front lines.

—Paulette Likoudis

Maps

Introduction & Acknowledgments

I grew up in central New York State, working long, hard hours in the dairy industry. I worked my way up to the position of herdsman and then specialized in herd management records.

Eventually, I saved enough to put myself through Cornell University's horseshoeing program, and then started my own draft horse business. I now employ myself full time as a farrier and blacksmith.

You could say my life has always been a series of hard work and long hours. But as I raised my family and pursued my many interests, one obsession I have always had was a keen interest in early American history.

I will not pretend to be any kind of skilled historian— I'm an amateur at best. In my studies, I ran across a theory and a story that I feel has to be told, and one I feel is far more accurate than what we've been told for centuries.

Any interest in the story of General Benedict Arnold came from links to my own family history. My family moved to central New York in 1722. They were Palatine German farmers.

My seven times great grandfather was burned out by the Mohawk Indians four times. His son served in the Tryon County militia and probably served—at least briefly—under General Arnold. Three of my family members died in the Battle of Oriskany.

In succeeding generations, one family member even married a Mohawk woman. So, family stories of early American history have always piqued my interest.

The story of General Benedict Arnold always intrigued me. His defection never made any kind of sense and I kept digging for truth and understanding.

I must acknowledge many real historians in my research, especially the very detailed work of historian James Kirby Martin. I also gleaned information from the Library of Congress, the historical archives of New York State and numerous sources I can't even remember over many years of research.

My family must also be thanked for putting up with my obsessions. Thanks go to the many friends who helped with research and encouraged me to write down and produce this historical novel, especially Gail Wagner, Paulette Likoudis and Lou Robinson.

This book is meant to be a novel based on history. Surely, it will be criticized, as any information that deviates from assumed facts of history would be. But I believe my theories of events are quite accurate and feel that they could be vigorously defended as truth.

CHAPTER ONE

Questions & Understanding the Times

In this book, two great and very different bulls were about to lock horns and only one would survive. As an amateur historian whose main interest is the Revolution, I've studied the life and times of Benedict Arnold and George Washington, reaching a far different conclusion than we were taught in our history books. The story that follows needs to be told.

My research began many years ago with a tour of the upstate New York home of General Philip Schuyler. He was the commander of the northern army. On the tour, I was told that at one time Washington accused Schuyler of treason, but couldn't make the charges stick.

It made me wonder if there was a pattern in Washington's character that we weren't told about. As I explored more into these characters of our early history, I found many different realities that awoke me to a whole new understanding. But to try understanding history, you need to put yourself in the mindset of what it was like to be an American colonist. We're so far removed from the realities of life in the late 1700s that it's almost impossible for people to imagine today what life was like back then. For most, life was about survival, even in the good times.

If you were cold, you needed to get near a fire, made with wood you cut by a handsaw or, most likely, with an ax. There was no running water in homes. If you needed water to cook or wash with, you drew it by bucket from a nearby spring, creek or river. Any warm water had to be heated over the fire. Any lighting at night was from your fire or from candles.

Wood floors and glass windows were luxuries of the middle and upper classes. If you traveled, the roads were pretty much mud and dirt trails. Some of the lucky few owned horses or oxen. The most common form of transportation for the average citizen was walking.

As there were no bathrooms, you went to an outhouse, outdoor latrine or into the woods whenever necessary. Poor sanitation led to disease, a major concern.

To eat, you grew and stored your own food. Every detail of life was labor intensive. If you owned a horse or team of oxen, pastures had to be created by clearing trees and brush by hand, digging and pulling stumps along the way. Fences were made of rails you cut and split yourself. Hay for animals was cut by hand with a grass scythe or sickle, then raked and dried.

If you were building a frame house, beam work was done with an ax or adze. Even shingles for the roof were cut and sawed by hand. You would contract with a local blacksmith for nails and hinges forged by hand. Most folks settled for dirt floors and no windows.

Language was also a major obstacle for early settlers. Many spoke English, but a significant number spoke German or French. Also, Native Americans had their own languages.

Unemployment was not a problem and certainly not an option. But a lack of employees was. Americans needed lots of cheap labor and our forefathers wrestled with the sins of slavery and indentured servitude.

Just consider our third president, Thomas Jefferson. We know he was a great thinker and inventor. But he had the luxury of time to accomplish what he did. To run and maintain his farm took a staff of 77 slaves and servants. For Jefferson to travel from his Monticello plantation to Washington—about 100 miles as the crow flies—took four days and three nights, with many river crossings.

Life in the 1770s was a heavily classed society. God help you if you were of the lower class. The middle class was looked down on by the upper class. The middle class dreamed of attaining the higher status. The upper class clung desperately to their wealth, power and privilege.

Almost all Americans had lived previously under monarchies, so they were completely used to dealing with aristocracy and accustomed to bowing to it. Our first Continental Congress was comprised of almost all upper class representatives, with only a few middle class citizens included.

But even through all the trials and tribulations of simple everyday life in early America, it was an exciting and booming time in our history. Life here was far different than anywhere else in the world. Men could work their way into owning land of their own and if you had a marketable trade or skill, you could move up in the world and create your own business. Citizens felt hopeful, as long as they were free to use their own hands to build a life.

These new Americans believed the British monarchy was in their way, milking society with territorial taxation. For that reason, some joined militia groups for the "cause" of liberty. But those were high ideals, even for those who had the time and assets to consider participation.

A Continental soldier most likely didn't join the army to serve the cause of liberty. He saw it as a chance for pay, food, ordinary clothing and promises of pensions or land grants in return for his service. When enlistments were up, most men couldn't wait to get back home. For all they knew, the budding government they were fighting for could be as tyrannical as the one they were fighting against.

The British Redcoats weren't the only danger a Continental soldier faced. At any given time, up to a third of the troops were out of action because of dysentery or small pox.

As the First Continental Congress met, the politics and infighting were fierce. The New England states were at the end of their rope and itching for a fight. The southern states weren't so sure. The notion of taking on England was almost an insane idea. How could they even consider raising and supplying an army? They weren't even sure they could hold the colonies together in one accord for any purposes.

CHAPTER TWO

Enter King George?

It was into this fray came George Washington, a delegate from Virginia. For a long time, Washington ranked among the middle class. He worked as a surveyor and served as an officer in the French and Indian War. He didn't really distinguish himself much during the war, but it gave him credibility as a soldier and officer.

George had much higher ambitions, and he hit the jackpot when he married his wife, Martha Dandridge Custis, a wealthy widow and sole holder of a huge estate plantation in Virginia. That marriage propelled him into a world of the privileged gentry and the very upper class of society.

As Washington attended the First Continental Congress, he knew that if there was to be a war and a new nation, the colonies would need a king or exalted ruler of some kind, and most likely, this ruler would come from the military side of events.

George Washington wanted that job badly. At his congressional appearances, he typically dressed in his old military uniform. At six feet and one inch tall, he was a very imposing figure, as the average man's height was much shorter.

He seemed to want to stay above the political fray and touted his experience at warfare. The New England delegations preferred the experience put forth by another gentleman named Horatio Gates. Gates had more experience and had served longer in the British military.

Delegates knew that holding the alliance of colonies together would be easier with a commander-in-chief from the south. Washington was the obvious choice and he made sure that was known. Washington's preferred title throughout the war was "His Excellency." George always traveled with one or more of his slaves and was of the elite class, as many in Congress expected from a military commander of the times.

Arnold was described as "handsome-faced, muscular, and well-made"
Oil painting of Benedict Arnold by Doug Henry. *Courtesy of the late
Bill Stanley, past president of the Norwich Historical Society.*

CHAPTER THREE

Arnold, A Natural Born Leader Ready for War

Benedict Arnold's background and life were far different than Washington's. His bloodlines traced back to the Puritans. His family arrived in Massachusetts in 1635.

William Arnold and his sons moved to Rhode Island and purchased vast tracts of land, close to 10,000 acres. They became some of the wealthiest settlers in early America. Benedict the First, William's oldest son, became the colony's governor.

William was held in high regard by the citizens, and upon his death in 1678, nearly 1,000 mourners attended his funeral.

In succeeding generations of Arnolds, the land was equally divided into smaller and smaller portions, as they believed in partible inheritance. By the time Benedict's father was of age, the Arnold clan—mostly farmers—were deemed solidly middle class families.

As a young man, Benedict's father knew he had a dwindling hope of any inheritance and he moved to Norwich, Connecticut with one of his brothers. He found employment as a cooper, making barrels, but he had hopes of entering the new, thriving Yankee mercantile trade.

Opportunity smiled on William upon his marriage to a wealthy widow, Hannah King. Her former husband was lost at sea and she inherited his trading business, which now through their marriage became William's family business. He became known around Norwich as the "Captain," through his trading ventures, which stretched as far as the West Indies.

Arnold's father bought five acres and a two-story house outside the village of Norwich and he became an upwardly-mobile leader in the community. The Arnolds enjoyed a happy marriage that produced six children. They were very religious and held tightly to their Puritan roots. They prayed together and wanted the very best for their children.

Around 12 or 13 years of age, Benedict was sent to boarding school to learn Latin, writing, mathematics and various other subjects. As he matured, his parents hoped to enter him in nearby Yale College. They valued education very highly, along with strict religious training.

Benedict was the oldest of the children. An older brother died at one year of age, before Benedict's birth.

A sister, Hannah, was a year younger than Benedict and his sister, Mary, was four years younger. Another brother, Absalom, was six years younger and his sister, Elizabeth, was eight years younger.

There were comments written about Benedict's great athletic ability, as he was one of the best skaters during the long New England winters. But young Benedict's ideal childhood didn't last very long. When he was about eleven, his brother, Absalom, died of an unknown illness. At age 12, while Benedict was in his studies at boarding school, an epidemic of diphtheria hit most of New England. Diphtheria was referred to as throat distemper and many children died a horrible death, unable to breathe and unable to fight high fever. The disease took the lives of Benedict's younger sisters, Mary and Elizabeth, their deaths only 19 days apart.

His father's business fell on hard times during the same period. Trading was slow due to warring superpowers in the Caribbean. The failing of business and the loss of children took a devastating toll on the family. Benedict's father couldn't hold up to the pressure and began drinking heavily, severely affecting his health and further destroying his business.

The Arnolds struggled to keep Benedict in school, as he was doing so well, but eventually could no longer afford the tuition. In this desperate situation, his mother, Hannah, reached out to her relatives, the Lathrops.

The Lathrops were upper class graduates of Yale. They were in the apothecary and trading businesses. They offered to take Benedict into their businesses as an apprentice. They noticed that he was a natural at business and considered him a model apprentice.

But young Benedict had to grow up quickly. Family matters turned even worse and by the time he was 18, his beloved and distressed mother passed away. His father became known for drinking in public, blemishing the family name. He was looked down on by the Norwich community. Benedict became responsible for attending to his father's failing health and the care of his remaining sister, Hannah, whom he was very close to.

By the time Benedict was 20, his father had died. Creditors pressed for debt payments and the family home had to be sold to settle them. If it weren't for the kindness of the Lathrops, he and his sister would have been destitute. Benedict threw his troubles into his work. He seemed determined to build back his family's name and he worked tirelessly for the Lathrops. They were so impressed with the young Arnold that they decided to expand their business and make him a junior partner in a new venture in New Haven, Connecticut.

That development meant a whole new life and beginning for Benedict and he couldn't wait for the opportunity. New Haven was some 50 miles away from Norwich and his troubled early life.

New Haven, the home of Yale College, was a boom town of the early colonies. Sailing ships constantly landed at the deep port and unloaded goods to be traded from there to New York City, Boston, the West Indies and England. Benedict could not have been more excited to set up shop there. With a loan from the Lathrops, Benedict began building an apothecary business. He became very popular among his clientele, as he knew what tough times were and gladly extended credit to those who needed it. He sold books, medicine, rum, sugar and many other items for "cash or short credit."

His customers thought highly of the intelligent young man and began referring to him as "Doctor Arnold." Benedict moved his sister, Hannah, to New Haven to help with the thriving new business.

The old guard families of New Haven got quite nervous about Benedict, because he was so bold and quick to criticize the tax policies of England. Through his need of supply and the Lathrops' connections with trade vessels, Benedict expanded into the lucrative merchant trading business. He formed a somewhat loose partnership with another young trader, Adam Babcock. It wasn't long before they were operating three ships.

Benedict continued his apothecary with the help of his sister, Hannah, but his drive and energy knew no bounds. He hired sailing crews and began commanding ships up and down the East coast, to the West Indies and all the way to Montreal. He traded in molasses, horses, rum, pork, grain and timber products. His trading and sea skills grew and he became one of the best traders in New England.

Men like John Hancock were in the same trade and they were outraged by the heavy tax burden imposed on them by Great Britain. Taxes were sucking the freedom and profit from their hard-earned businesses. The trading business was truly hard-earned. Besides having to put together business deals, owners managed crews of men, staffed ships and faced dangerous storms while traveling up and down the coast. Giving up their profits to Great Britain was a very hard pill to swallow.

Benedict was not known as an easygoing person. When he was in the right, he was quick-tempered and if you dared to question his integrity or honor, you'd better be prepared to duel, fight or be publicly humiliated. He was a natural leader. Men gravitated to him and respected his strength of character.

The shipping trade finely honed Benedict's skills as a sea captain. Trading in horses turned him into an excellent horseman and expert rider.

In 1765, tensions between the colonies and Great Britain were beginning to surface. The straw that was breaking the colonists' spirit was the imposition of the

Stamp Act. The government insisted stamps be placed on some 50 items, including newspapers, pamphlets, wills, land deeds, college diplomas and port clearance papers for all trading vessels. British regulars were sent to enforce the law and punish smugglers.

Groups of resistors, such as the Sons of Liberty, began to spring up. Men considered to be agitators—like Boston's Samuel Adams—organized resistance through intimidation, causing the Stamp Act to be ineffective.

In Connecticut, Jared Ingersoll, who served as Benedict's lawyer and whom Benedict knew well, was named as a Stamp Act distributor. On a trip to Hartford, Ingersoll was surrounded by the Sons of Liberty. They made him sign a sworn statement renouncing any intention of administering the Stamp Act. He was also forced to throw his hat in the air and say he would reject Parliament's tax plan in favor of "liberty and property," with three cheers. Onlookers shouted "huzzah." After that, no one would step forward to be a Stamp Act distributor.

The Stamp Act and the threat of the act curtailed a significant amount of trading in New England and threw the area into a severe depression. Benedict's creditors called him to account, and at one point, his debts were a bit higher than his net worth. He made an agreement to settle the terms, but came close to bankruptcy and debtor's prison. He had to become much more careful about extending credit to his customers. After almost losing his business, Benedict honed his skills as a businessman.

Men like Arnold and Hancock had to resort to attempting to smuggle goods to avoid the heavy taxation that was crippling businesses and destroying profits.

On one occasion, a seaman attempted to threaten Benedict with blackmail, saying if he wasn't paid a substantial sum he would notify the tax authorities that Benedict was unloading molasses without paying the three cent per gallon tax. Benedict wasn't going to put up with such behavior, especially from one of his own men. He took his crew and found the man in a local tavern, pushed him out into the street, had him whipped publicly and ordered him to leave New Haven and never to return.

That action succeeded in keeping the colonists from siding with British authorities, but greatly upset the old guard authority of New Haven. They called Benedict to account for disrupting order and fined him 50 pounds, which he paid, but he had also gotten his point across.

British loyalists became very nervous, as Benedict delivered public speeches about the merits of liberty. Many citizens were whipped into a frenzy, burning prominent old guard characters in effigy. After that demonstration, Benedict was known as man not be taken lightly. In 1767, he put aside his financial troubles and began speaking up for liberty.

Benedict then fell in love with and married Margaret "Peggy" Mansfield. She was the daughter of a local merchant, Samuel Mansfield, who was also acting sheriff in New Haven County. Over the next five years, Benedict and Peggy had three sons. Benedict VI was born in 1768; Richard in 1769 and Henry in 1772.

It was good marriage, but definitely strained. Benedict was fiercely determined to make his business successful. He was away from home many months at a time, which made Peggy resentful. She worked with Benedict's sister, Hannah, to handle some of the business dealings while busy raising the couple's sons.

By 1770, Benedict had grown his business, trading goods from the West Indies to Canada and all of New England. In a short time, he became one of the wealthiest merchants in New England. In 1770, he built for Peggy a beautiful two-story house with three acres on Water Street in New Haven. There were formal gardens, stables and a coach house. Benedict was very proud of his new home, one of the best in New Haven. It was a comfortable abode for his wife, children and his sister, Hannah.

The same year Benedict built his new house, the Boston Massacre occurred. British soldiers fired on a mob in Boston and were arrested for murder.

Britain was oppressive over the issue of taxation because the Seven Years War with Spain and France had

Arnold was proud of the new home he built in
Newhaven on Water Street. The house had formal gardens
and a carriage house. *Courtesy, Library of Congress.*

doubled her national debt. The mother country was
desperate to raise funds to pay creditors. The colonies
were seen as a source of funding. Britain considered the
colonies to be unruly children who owed the parent
nation for stability and protection.

By 1773 and 1774, tensions in the colonies—especially
in New England—had reached a boiling point. In December of 1773, Samuel Adams addressed a crowd of
some 8,000 to protest the tax on tea. That demonstration brought on the Boston Tea Party.

A very angry British Parliament passed the first series of
Coercive Acts around March 1774. Essentially, Boston
Harbor was shut down until the tax on the dumped

tea was paid. By May 1774, Boston was put under the military rule of General Thomas Gage, commander of all British forces in the Colonies.

British troops set out to end self-rule by the colonists. By June of 1774, the Quartering Act required all colonists to provide housing for British troops by allowing them to occupy houses, taverns and any unoccupied buildings. Britain was determined to crush the rebellion.

The First Continental Congress met in the fall of 1774. The delegates knew the drums of war were beating. Fifty-six delegates, including the well-known George Washington, Samuel Adams, John Hancock, Patrick Henry and others, took action.

The delegates decided that Britain's Coercive Acts were not to be obeyed. The colonists wanted self rule, which they believed included life, liberty and property. They also agreed to boycott all English imports.

Benedict was more than ready to fight for the cause of liberty by late 1774. He helped form a local militia of about 65 men, in New Haven. Those supporters voted to name Benedict as their captain. They were provided a few new, blue uniforms for the rebels to wear—probably paid for by Benedict—as they drilled in preparation for war.

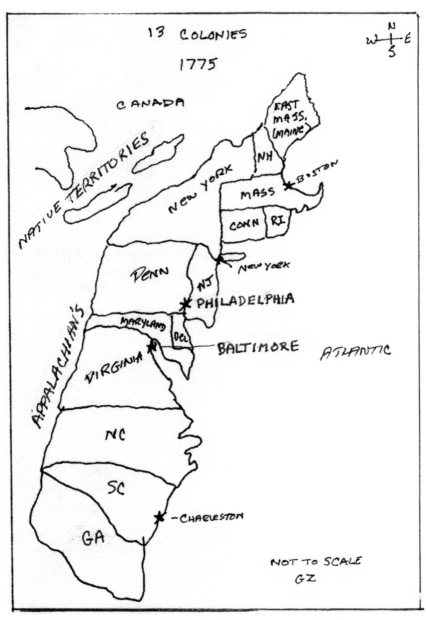

The Thirteen Colonies.

CHAPTER FOUR

The War Begins

In April of 1775, Massachusetts Governor Thomas Gage was secretly ordered by Britain to suppress the open rebellion. He ordered 700 British soldiers to march on Concord to destroy the colonists' weapons depot. His action sparked the Midnight Ride of Paul Revere. John Hancock and Samuel Adams were hiding near Lexington and got the message.

At the dawn of April 19, 1775, about 70 brave militiamen went toe to toe with the advance guard of the British force on Lexington Green. The "shot heard around the world" was fired. The war was on.

The British did manage to destroy the weapons depot at Concord, but suffered the loss of 250 men on their retreat back to Boston. The news spread quickly—for the times—and militia from all over New England were called on to lay siege to British-held Boston.

When the news reached Benedict in New Haven, he quickly assembled his men. They agreed to muster and leave for Boston the next morning. Benedict also accepted a few volunteer students from Yale University to help fill the ranks.

The next morning, Benedict's small column received a blessing and prayers from the local reverend. People in town gathered to cheer the group on. All they were lacking were a few more weapons and they needed access to the town powder magazine.

Town authorities and prominent old guard figures were meeting at a tavern. They held the keys to the magazine. They weren't sure they wanted to get involved with this fight and wanted to get more details of what went on in Lexington and Concord. They sent a message to Benedict stating he couldn't have the keys to the powder magazine, nor could he have permission to run to Massachusetts.

Benedict then assembled his men in front of the tavern and demanded the keys, saying, "None but Almighty God shall prevent my marching." Benedict gave the keepers of the magazine five minutes to make their decision. They had no choice but to relent.

Once supplied, Benedict's boldness must have inspired the whole town. Most of them turned out to cheer the group of soldiers with a flurry of huzzahs as they tromped toward Boston. Along their march to Boston, Benedict's small force—probably around a nighttime campfire—gathered and wrote a pledge. It provided a good insight of their character and mindset. It was quite unusual for the times.

They wrote: "Driven to our last necessity and obliged to have recourse to arms in defense of our lives and liberties." They promised, "To conduct ourselves decently and inoffensively as we march, both to our countrymen and to one another, renouncing drunkenness, gaming, profaneness and every vice of that nature. Serving in such a great and glorious cause."

Also included in their intentions was a curious phrase that showed their Christian and Puritan roots. They wrote that the guidelines would go to "all Christian people believing in and relying on that God, to whom our enemies have at last forced us to appease."

Many other militia groups were covertly planning and marching to a confrontation with the Redcoats at Boston, giving up their families, their wives, their businesses, properties and the safety of their homes. Some were traveling from as far away as Virginia.

Benedict's men arrived in Cambridge by April 29, 1775. But along the march, Benedict had a meeting that would take him in a completely different direction. He met during his journey with a Colonel Samuel Parsons, also a Connecticut patriot. Parsons was returning to Connecticut with orders to recruit more troops.

Parsons informed Benedict of the dire situation around Boston and the extreme need for more ordnance, especially cannons, to drive the British forces out of Boston. In their discussion, Benedict pointed out that there were a large number of cannons that could be seized at Fort Ticonderoga on Lake Champlain. From his trading ventures in the Montreal area, he knew the old fort was lightly manned.

Benedict, with his business background, knew things didn't get accomplished by talking about them. He was a vigorous and extreme man of actions. Parsons, excited about Benedict's information, went directly to Hartford and met with the provincial leaders there. They saw the value of launching an immediate strike on Fort Ticonderoga. Funds were withdrawn from their treasury and Captain Edward Mott was appointed to head the strike. Herman Allen was asked to get in touch with his brother, Ethan, to enlist the help of the Green Mountain Boys.

The trek to Fort Ticonderoga was started on April 29, 1775; the same day Benedict's men arrived in Cambridge. Upon his arrival at Cambridge, Benedict provided accommodations for his men, probably supplied by money out of his own pocket. He immediately sought out Dr. Joseph Warren and other members of the Massachusetts Committee of Safety to convince them that he needed to launch a campaign to secure the ordnance at Fort Ticonderoga.

On May 2, 1775, the Committee of Safety named Benedict colonel of a force not to exceed 400 men. They would rely on his "judgment, fidelity and valor" for a secret mission to capture Fort Ticonderoga. They also supplied him with a cash amount of 100 pounds currency, two hundred pounds of gunpowder, 1,000 flints for muskets, lead musket balls and ten horses. Along with his written orders, Benedict was authorized to draw on the committee's credit for provisions needed by the small army.

Benedict knew that time was of the essence since the British would be moving to reinforce the garrisons of the Lake Champlain region. He was not a patient man—armies moved much too slowly for his liking. As he rode west through Massachusetts, Benedict was probably thinking of the acclaim he would receive if he could capture Fort Ticonderoga and its ordnance. He made the decision to ride ahead of his men. They knew where they were going, but he just couldn't wait any longer. He rode day and night at breakneck speed toward Fort Ticonderoga.

Along the journey, Benedict got word of the Mott and Allen venture already in progress. He was likely hoping to ask the Green Mountain Boys to join his men.

He heard they were meeting at Remington's Tavern in Castleton. Benedict arrived too late for the meeting, but some of the rear guard of the Green Mountain Boys were still at the tavern.

Benedict showed them his orders from the Massachusetts Committee of Safety and informed them he intended to lead the command of the strike force. They probably weren't that impressed, as all Benedict had were some papers and an army, days behind. They told him Allen was their leader, and that they were gathering at Shoreham, the starting point of the attack.

Exhausted from his ride, Benedict spent the night at the tavern and early on morning of May 9 left for Shoreham, hoping to take command of the Mott and Allen strike.

The Green Mountain Boys were a renegade militia movement based in the mountains of Vermont and New Hampshire. They were a very rugged group of farm settlers who had banded together for their own protection. In today's vernacular, they would be known as mountain warlords. They had no qualms about carrying out raids on Loyalist properties. There was even a reward posted by the Governor of New York for Ethan Allen's head, as a result of raids conducted across the border. The Green Mountain Boys were hoping the capture of Fort Ticonderoga would give them legitimacy as part of the patriot coalition.

Fort Ticonderoga was a large fortress originally positioned by the French in 1755 to fortify the Lake Champlain region. That region, stretching from Canada through the Richelieu River to Lake Champlain to Lake George to the Hudson River to Albany to New York City, was the main travel and supply chain from north to south in the colonies' rough interior. There weren't many roads, but the route would be the equivalent of Route I-95 today. A number of small fortresses protected the Champlain region. Fort Ticonderoga was the oldest and largest fort on the lake.

Benedict caught up with the Mott and Allen contingent about noon that very day, May 9. There was much friction at first, but Benedict claimed command by holding legitimate paperwork issued by the Massachusetts Committee of Safety. However, the Green Mountain Boys weren't going to be led by anyone but Ethan Allen. When the dust settled, all agreed to a joint command. Benedict's small army was on the way, but days behind. Fort Ticonderoga was still very lightly garrisoned.

There were many accounts—favoring one or the other—of how the meeting of Allen and Benedict went down. One report stated that Ethan was in his tent, despondent over how the fort could be attacked, when Benedict burst in and shoved him around, saying, "We're not only going to the fort, but we're going to do it tonight!"

As Benedict waved his papers around, it could have been where the phrase "you and what army" originated. The best guess is that Ethan and Benedict reached a mutual agreement.

While all of this was going on, the Second Continental Congress was meeting in Philadelphia. The delegates elected John Hancock as president of the congress and George Washington as commander-in-chief of the new Continental American Army.

But the delegates didn't make any snap decisions. It took them from May 10, 1775 to June 15 to agree on a state of defense, who would lead and other details. Benedict and other patriots were already fully engaged in the war. Regardless of how events unfolded at Fort Ticonderoga, it was a surprise attack.

CHAPTER FIVE

America's First Victory

At approximately four in the morning, under darkness, only one sentry was on duty. Allen and Benedict led the charge through the gates and into the parade ground. The lone sentry rushed to get help, but the whole garrison was caught completely off guard. It turned out to be a bloodless victory. By the time British commander Captain William Delaplace was awakened, the successful attack was nearly over. He surrendered to Allen and Benedict, negotiating prisoner of war rights for his 44 men, 24 women and children.

Much to Benedict's disgust, the Green Mountain Boys found 90 gallons of rum and proceeded to celebrate their victory, getting very drunk and looting the fort. He knew that once they sobered up and had their fill of loot, they would disappear back to the mountains, as they all had crops to attend to.

Two days later, the rebels took a smaller fort to the north, known as Crown Point. It, too, fell easily since it was garrisoned by only nine British regulars. Within four days, the Green Mountain Boys began slipping home in small groups with what loot they could find and some of Benedict's men began filtering into the area.

By the 14th of May 1775, Benedict no longer had a disputed claim to command. His army had finally caught up with him. With his victories, he secured 201 artillery pieces, with over 100 in good, usable condition.

But resting wasn't in Benedict's vocabulary. He was already making plans to secure the whole Champlain region. Opportunity knocked when a good sized schooner—owned by a wealthy, confirmed Loyalist—was captured in Skenesborough by the Green Mountain Boys on their way to Fort Ticonderoga. They turned it over to Eleazer Oswald, a good friend of Benedict's. They knew little about sailing, so it was of no use to them.

Benedict couldn't wait to get his sea legs back again. Because of his trading ventures, there wasn't anything about sailing he didn't know. He had the schooner fitted with two cannons, six swivel guns and renamed the ship "Liberty." America's first war ship sailed north toward Canada, accompanied by bateaus found in the area. Bateaus were small, flat-bottomed craft similar to rowboats. They could be rowed or pulled along rivers.

Sometimes they were improvised with small sails to lessen rowing.

The tiny navy sailed north with an objective. Benedict knew that in the area there was a main supply ship used by the British to transport troops and goods to forts along Lake Champlain. That mission alone should have given Benedict credit as the father of the American Navy.

At the lake's end, Benedict selected 35 of his best, most able men. They rowed all night and made a surprise raid at St. Johns, where the British supply sloop was moored. The small British garrison was caught completely off guard. The sloop, more bateaus and two more cannons were secured for America. In addition, 20 Redcoats were captured as prisoners.

They sailed off with their prizes and destroyed any remaining transport the British had stored there before British reinforcements could arrive from Montreal. Now, even if the Brits wanted to attack the southern forts on the lake, they would have to build ships and bateaus first. America's first little navy now controlled the whole lake region.

As Benedict sailed south, he met up with Ethan Allen and about 100 of the Green Mountain Boys. They were rowing hard to try and catch up with Benedict and had dreams of more plunder at St. Johns. Benedict gave them some more food, which they were in short supply of.

Benedict invited Allen aboard ship and tried to make amends for stepping on toes a few days earlier. They had a drink together and toasted the Second Continental Congress that was meeting in Philadelphia. Allen decided he wanted to go on to St. Johns with his boys. Benedict told him there was no point to his mission. They had already captured the ships, and surely, British reinforcements would be coming down from Montreal.

Allen, being quite strong-willed himself, wanted to go on to raid any remaining supplies in the St. Johns area. Benedict continued south and was found to be correct. By the time Allen's men got to St. Johns, they ran into a column of 200 British regulars coming in to reinforce the area. As Allen's men faced cannon fire and grapeshot, somehow most of them escaped and made their way back down the lake with their tails between their legs. That failure furthered Benedict's reputation as a superior commander and left Ethan Allen a little embarrassed and jealous.

As an experienced ship commander who was very detail oriented, Benedict set about readying his troops at Fort Ticonderoga with regular drills and discipline. He refitted the captured British ship and renamed it "Enterprise." He also readied the captured cannons for the trip back to Boston.

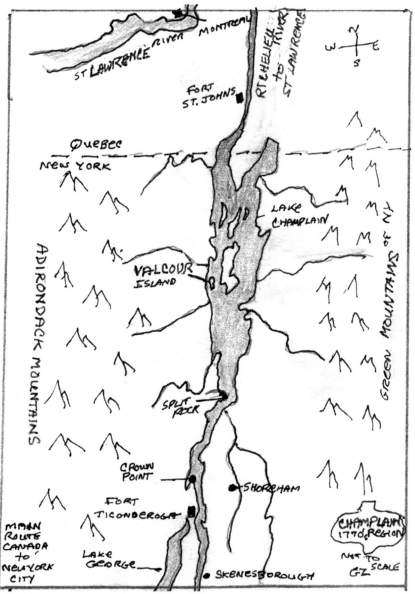

Champlain Region

The loss of the whole Champlain region and the corridor from Canada to the south was a huge embarrassment for Great Britain. British Governor Carlton in Canada wrote to England that some "horse jockey" named Arnold had led the rout of the area.

The Second Continental Congress was made quite upset by Benedict's actions. They supposed themselves to be in a defensive posture in America, but Benedict had made the situation into an offensive war by openly striking British strongholds all the way to Canada. Many moderate congressmen were doing more than just a little hand wringing. Their hope of reconciliation with Great Britain was slipping away. Also, as politics often go, others were trying to suppress Benedict's reputation and take credit for themselves.

Benedict was learning the hard way that merits and actions alone weren't enough to win acclaim. Politics in the early Revolution was a vicious dog-eat-dog business that Benedict wasn't accustomed to. Each state had its own militias and individuals seeking glory for themselves. There was no unified mission or government yet.

By June 10th of 1775, the wrangling reached its boiling point in the field. Benedict was returning from a scouting mission on Champlain to his temporary headquarters at Crown Point. He was confronted by Ethan Allen, James Easton and some of the Green Mountain Boys. Allen announced himself as legitimate commander of the region. Easton, a tavern keeper with military aspirations, carried out-of-date papers with instructions from the Massachusetts Congress.

Benedict held his temper and said he was willing to give up command when anyone with proper authority appeared to take it. Allen and Easton had to step back because all the soldiers were clearly backing Benedict.

The next morning, all hell broke loose. Allen's party intended to leave the fortifications without "showing their passes" to the sentry. Easton hurled insults at Benedict. He reached his breaking point, which wasn't that high to begin with. Easton, who was armed with a cutlass and pistols, was grabbed by Benedict, who demanded that Easton "draw like a gentleman." He considered Easton a lying, dishonest coward.

When Easton declined to fight, Benedict "kicked him very heartily" and threw him out of camp. Thoroughly humiliated, Allen and Easton would prove to be Benedict's enemies in the political ring. Benedict's bravado and strength of character would rub many the wrong way throughout the war, although his men respected and loved him for it.

The political wrangling also reached its peak that summer. The Massachusetts Committee of Safety that had enlisted Benedict was worried they might not be able to continue financial support of his mission to Fort

Ticonderoga, even though Benedict was using much of his own funds for paying soldiers and buying supplies. That required extending and using his own credit. The committee knew he would have to eventually submit an account for reimbursement.

The Committee of Safety sent out a delegation to get information and review the situation. They were under pressure to relieve Benedict of his duties. Many wondered why a second-class merchant from Connecticut was commanding Massachusetts soldiers. Also, others like Easton and Allen were attacking his good name. Benedict was holding on, hoping to hear the intentions of the new Continental Congress, especially what they intended to do about pending British offensives through Canada.

If you think our forefathers acted harmoniously and in one accord, you would be mistaken. Many reconciliation-minded members of the congress were actually nervous and embarrassed about Allen and Benedict's actions. A majority of the congress voted to withdraw from the Champlain region and give its control back to Britain.

Benedict thought his actions would win him acclaim and couldn't believe the decisions made by the congress. In one letter to the congress, he wrote that their decisions "have thrown the inhabitants into the greatest confusion." At least 500 American families resided in the area and pulling out of the conflict would leave them at the mercy of the Redcoats and hostile Indians. He also wrote about Fort Ticonderoga: "the key of this extensive country, and if abandoned, leaves a very extensive frontier open to the ravages of the enemy and to continual alarms which will probably cost more than the expense of repairing and garrisoning it."

Luckily, due to Benedict's assessments, concerns from the Massachusetts congress and the rest of New England states that knew the importance of the Champlain corridor, the congress relented and reversed its decision.

In late June of 1775, Benedict decided to resign his commission, "not being able to hold it longer with honor." On hearing the news of Benedict's resignation, his men panicked for a short time. They needed his leadership desperately and many feared not getting paid for their service, as they had families to feed at home. They went as far as holding Benedict captive aboard the Liberty, at least until the pay issue was resolved by the Massachusetts Committee of Safety. Benedict held no ill well toward the action taken by his men and expressed as much. He knew what they were going through.

Benedict got news of the formation of a Continental Northern Army Department, under the command of Philip Schuyler of Albany, in early July of 1775. Schuyler was a well-known patriot serving in congress. He was a huge landowner in the area and a member of the elite class. He lived on a large estate near Albany. Benedict resolved to meet with Schuyler to give him intelligence about the Champlain region and maybe even offer his services.

On July 4th of 1775, Benedict left the Champlain region. One of his last statements to the new command at Fort Ticonderoga was that he wanted them to make sure they fortified Mount Defiance, a mountain that loomed over the old fort. He believed the Brits could haul cannons to its summit and force a surrender of Fort Ticonderoga. They should have taken his advice.

As an insight to what kind of leader and commander Benedict was, it must have warmed his heart when in an unprecedented show of affection, local residents gathered at Crown Point to say goodbye and wish him well. They handed him a proclamation of "Gratitude and Thankfulness," for the uncommon vigilance, vigor and spirit he displayed in "providing for our preservation and safety from the threatened and much dreaded incursions of an inveterate enemy."

The residents praised Benedict's "humanity and benevolence in supplying them with provisions in their distress." They also lauded his "polite manner" and "generosity of soul, which nothing less than real magnanimity and innate virtue could inspire." They wished that he would receive rewards "adequate to your merit."

Benedict made quite a good impression on the average people and they wanted him to know how much his good service meant to them. In fact, the only time that Benedict can be recalled severely disciplining his men was when two of them were caught looting residents' homes and he had them flogged for the offense. He always insisted that citizens be treated fairly and respectfully. That was surely not the Benedict portrayed throughout history.

CHAPTER SIX

War Growing Throughout New England

While Benedict was busy securing the Champlain region, the siege of Boston was growing in strength every day. On June 17, 1775, the Battle of Bunker Hill exploded. Two thousand British regulars tried to assault American forces and dug in on Breed's Hill. They succeeded on their third attempt, but suffered massive losses. Half—nearly 1,000 men—died in that battle. In comparison, about 400 Americans were lost, including General Joseph Warren of Massachusetts, a rebel friend of Benedict who had helped him secure his colonel's commission from the Massachusetts Committee of Safety.

When Benedict finally left Lake Champlain for Albany, George Washington was just arriving at Cambridge, across the river from Boston. The Continental Congress had just named him commander-in-chief of the new American army and he took charge of nearly 17,000 patriots in the surrounding area of Boston.

Benedict wasn't sure what to expect as he arrived at Philip Schuyler's home in Albany. Schuyler was of the very upper class of New York, a wealthy landowner and skilled politician known as an aristocratic gentleman. Schuyler had just returned home from serving in the Continental Congress and had also just received his appointment as Northern Army commander.

To Benedict's surprise, Schuyler was actually anxious to meet him. The fame earned by Benedict for his Champlain exploits was spreading. Schuyler knew from field reports that Benedict was a man who could get things done. He warmly welcomed Benedict and was hoping to enlist him as an adjunct general in his division. He had very few leaders he could rely on as men of action.

Benjamin Hinman, the commander of the Committee of Safety left in charge of Fort Ticonderoga, was already labeled "king log" for his inability to make command decisions. Schuyler needed to pick Benedict's experiences to ascertain information about the Champlain region.

Benedict suggested that while there was still time in the campaign year before the onset of winter, they should launch a strike at the Canadian posts before the British could further reinforce them. He feared that if reinforced outposts gained too much strength, a British campaign down Lake Champlain might be launched and split the communication and supply lines of the colonies. Benedict also felt from his dealings and trade business in Canada, that the country to the north might even be willing to join the American cause for liberty.

As Schuyler and Benedict conferred on plans about whether or not they should take an offensive or defensive posture, Benedict received shocking news from Connecticut. His wife, Peggy, and his father-in-law had both died in June.

Benedict's grief was unbearable. He had three children to care for and he started for home. His wife was barely 30 years old and he missed his children and home terribly. Most men would have been crushed under such devastating news. He certainly had done more than his share in the cause. Most would have said that's enough.

Over the next two and a half months, Benedict was in severe despair when he visited the gravesites of his dear Peggy and father-in-law. His sister, Hannah, did her utmost to bring Benedict back to his feet. She loved her brother and his children dearly. She agreed to be their surrogate mother and try to keep Benedict's mercantile business affairs running as smoothly as she could. Benedict felt he could best submerge his sorrows in "consideration of the public cause."

Besides all of the business and personal problems Benedict had to face at home, he still needed to make his way back to the Committee of Safety in Massachusetts to settle his expenses for the Ticonderoga campaign. He also thought that as long as he were there, he would present himself to the new commander-in-chief, George Washington, and maybe offer his service.

Much weighed on Benedict's mind as he prepared to head back to Massachusetts. One of his main sources of income, the merchant ship Peggy—named for his wife—had just cleared New Haven's port, en route to Quebec. Now that the area was a potential war zone, he feared the British might seize the craft.

Benedict's three sons—the oldest of whom was only seven—surely didn't want their father to leave again.

Riding horseback to the Massachusetts Provincial Congress, Benedict arrived there on August 1st of 1775. He presented his documented expenses and accounts for the Ticonderoga mission. As politics often go, there were many disputes over the claims. Only about half of what Benedict submitted was reimbursed. Later on in the war, the Continental Congress—shamed by the shabby treatment of such a patriot—ponied up funds to cover more of his expenses.

CHAPTER SEVEN

The Two Bulls Meet

In mid-August, Benedict and Washington finally met in Cambridge. Washington had his hands full after just receiving command of some 17,000 patriot troops on July 3rd. They certainly weren't a cohesive army, but a mix of militia groups and some enlisted regulars. The logistics of defenses, food, supplies, discipline and supply lines must have been overwhelming.

Washington was constantly thirsty for information. He always tried to calculate his moves based on having as much intelligence as he could gather. He was eager to meet this Benedict Arnold, whose reputation had preceded him. While in Champlain, Benedict had sent regular reports to the Continental Congress, where Washington was serving.

In his reports, Benedict had tried to encourage the Congress to back a campaign striking into Canada before that country could be reinforced by the British.

Washington had read the reports while serving in the Congress, and was of the same opinion as Benedict. He was also amazed by Benedict's conquests around Lake Champlain. Both men feared the impending doom that was about to come down upon America from the northern corridor.

If the Brits controlled the St. Lawrence River and fortified Quebec and Montreal, they could easily go south through Champlain to Lake George and onto the Hudson River. That scenario not only would separate the colonies, but would disrupt all communications and supply lines, probably destroying any hope for independence.

Washington continued to be in awe of Benedict's knowledge and penetrating mind, when it came to military matters. Benedict knew many Canadians well through his merchant trading ventures in the area. He also was familiar with all the waterways going south and had already proved he was the kind of man to get things accomplished.

The two men summarized, after much discussion, that a two-pronged attack in Quebec might be the best way to thwart the British before they could reinforce the region in the spring. They needed to move very quickly. Washington and Benedict thought that if a force could travel through Maine and if Schuyler could send a force north from Albany, they could converge on Quebec. If they could gain control of Quebec and the St. Lawrence, they might have a chance at stopping the British.

Washington and Benedict were also counting on many freedom-loving Canadians eager to join the rebellion. Some of those even went so far as forming a delegation to go to the Congress as a 14th colony.

The two leaders also knew there would be much resistance from the French Canadian Catholic population. That group would have to be won over, since many of them had no trust of the New England Protestants. Another factor to be considered was the large contingent of Native Americans in the area. Some were friendly and some were not. Most were indifferent to either side, as they were just trying to survive in such a harsh country.

Summer was waning into fall and time was pressing, if the plan was to be launched. Washington wrote an express letter to Schuyler, his northern commander, explaining his intentions and requesting an immediate answer. He also knew Benedict would be the most logical choice to lead the Maine expedition.

Schuyler responded favorably to the plan, already confident of Benedict's abilities. He wrote: "How happy" he was "to learn of your intentions and wished the thought had struck you sooner." Washington offered Benedict a colonel's commission and put him in charge of the Maine expedition. They started planning the endeavor feverishly.

Washington knew of a shipbuilder named Reuben Colburn who had come to Cambridge from Maine with some St. Francis Indians—the Indians living in the vicinity of Quebec. They were familiar with the Kennebec River system. Washington needed to put Benedict in touch with Colburn.

Benedict penned a note to Colburn on August 21st, inquiring if he could "procure or build" 200 bateaus at his shipyard. Each would require four oars, two paddles, two setting poles and be capable of carrying six or seven men, along with their provisions and baggage. He also asked about the availability of "fresh beef" and "particular information" on the wilderness route to Quebec.

With Washington's permission, Colburn hurried to his shipyard in Gardinerston, Maine to begin filling the rush order. On September 3rd, Washington sent an express letter to Colburn, formally ordering the construction of 200 bateaus, at the rate of 40 shillings per craft. He additionally asked Colburn to gather food, supplies and up to 20 men who could serve as guides and carpenters qualified to repair the small boats as they traveled through the wilderness.

On September 2nd, a message was sent to Nathaniel Tracy—a wealthy merchant in Newburyport, Massachusetts—asking that he gather enough vessels to transport a "body of troops" on "a secret expedition." Men needed to be moved up the coast from Newburyport to Gardinerston at the headwater of the Kennebec River.

With many logistics of their plan coming together, Washington called on September 5th for "volunteers," saying he needed experienced woodsmen and men familiar with bateaus. The next morning brought a flood of volunteers for the mission. Many were sick of the boredom and disease of camp life, especially since things were progressing so slowly under the new command around Boston. Some wanted to serve under Benedict because of his growing reputation.

The list of volunteers, including Christopher Greene, Henry Dearborn and Aaron Burr, would impress most historians. But by far, the most impressive part of Benedict's force was three groups of Pennsylvania and Virginia frontiersmen. The Virginia forces under the command of Daniel Morgan were fierce backwoods fighters. They went to Cambridge, marching 600 miles in three weeks.

The two Pennsylvania forces under William Hendrix and Matt Smith covered some 450 miles in 26 days. They carried tomahawks and scalping knives. They were equipped with long rifles and were renowned as excellent marksmen.

But, these men weren't prone to the kind of discipline that Washington expected from his troops. They drank hard, fought hard and had a tendency to start fights in camp, just for fun. Washington was very glad to see these men included in the military effort and was glad to see them leave his command. Benedict knew they were the kind of men he needed for this mission to succeed.

The men chosen were all young, strong men who could move quickly through the wilderness. They would be the equivalent of today's Army Rangers. Benedict's force now numbered 1,050. The demand for supplies was a nightmare. Besides the bateaus being built in Maine, there was the list of food, supplies, gunpowder and transport issues.

Benedict hurried to cover every detail. He enlisted Dr. Isaac Senter, a surgeon from New Hampshire; Reverend Samuel Spring as chaplain; and Eleanor Oswald, a personal secretary who was an old friend from Ticonderoga. The troops were outfitted with new coats, linen frocks and blankets. Benedict also checked and attended to the firearms, flints, gunpowder and tents.

Daniel Morgan and Benedict quickly became friends and took command of the three rifle companies within the division. Morgan was a huge man and wasn't afraid to enforce his orders with his fist, if necessary. Curiously, two very brave women accompanied their husbands. Possibly, going to war with a loved one was almost better than trying to survive alone in colonial times.

Daniel Morgan was a huge man who ruled his riflemen with his fists.
He fought his way across Maine with Benedict, was with him in battle at
Quebec, Saratoga, and Yorktown. He later served in Congress.
Courtesy, Library of Congress

CHAPTER EIGHT

Mission Impossible, 1775 Style

Benedict had managed to organize and ready the mission in less than one month. The men assembled in Newburyport, Massachusetts for the first leg of the journey by September 17th. Waiting were eleven sloops and schooners ready to make the voyage to Maine. A strong headwind prevented the launch for two days.

Benedict rode among the troops, offering words of encouragement, but the men were anxious to get on with the mission. The wind finally calmed enough and Benedict had the men loaded onto the ships on September 19th.

As they left, there was a celebration of fifes and drums and many huzzahs. Also, shouts of "To Quebec and victory!" It would be the last happy days they would see for a long time. If they knew what was ahead on this mission of legends, none would have gone.

They set sail into the Atlantic. The sea was choppy and fog rolled in. Many men succumbed to seasickness, but they made it over some 100 miles to the coast of Maine in 12 hours. The voyage saved them close to six days of marching. As they picked their way through the many islands near the mouth of the Kennebec River, some of the ships went off course and that held them up another day. They finally arrived at Colburn's shipyard on September 22nd.

Colburn's men had worked day and night to finish the rush order of 200 bateaus. Many were hastily put together with green lumber and they were smaller than requested. To accommodate all the men and supplies, another 20 bateaus were needed. Colburn managed to put together more boats in three days. The carpenters who were asked to go along on the trek would certainly be needed, as these crafts would need repairs.

As Benedict waited for Colburn and his men to get ready for the next leg of the journey, he studied his scouting reports. They were truly going into an unknown wilderness. The Kennebec River is a fast flowing, deep river, filled with rapids and waterfalls. It runs quickly from the high Maine mountains to the Atlantic, with tremendous force. Most would not want to cross many places with a small boat, let alone pulling loaded boats upstream.

Benedict had crude maps and scouting reports he had requested prior to the mission. What he didn't know was how inaccurate the reports were. The journey was estimated to be 180 miles, but clearly it was close to 350. The scouts were troubled by the thought of encountering bands of Mohawk Indians, especially since they would have to cross the lands belonging to the warrior, "Chief Natanis." They weren't sure how this army's intrusion would be received.

Sending his men upriver in waves, Benedict's first group was Daniel Morgan's riflemen. They were to scout out the route and make pathways for portages around the raging rapids and waterfalls. The rest followed with the food stores and supplies. The first group set out on September 25th. Over the next four days, Benedict sent three more divisions into the wilderness. Benedict set out on September 29th, following from the rear.

One event took time from the many details Benedict had to oversee. A young soldier, James McCormick, got terribly drunk just before embarking and shot another soldier dead. His division held a court martial and sentenced him to death by hanging. The accused man broke down at the gallows. Benedict took pity on him and described McCormick as "very simple and ignorant" and normally a "peaceable fellow" and a "proper object of mercy." He made arrangements to send the disgraced soldier back to Cambridge for trial.

This painting depicts a portage on the wild Kennebec River, and gives an idea of the bateaus used in the epic journey through the Maine wilderness. *Courtesy, Library of Congress.*

As Benedict entered the mighty Kennebec River, he was glad to finally have his whole force in motion. He hoped to advance from the rear to the lead of the column, within four or five days. He traveled in a dugout canoe with his friend, Eleazer Oswald, and some Indian guides.

As he made his way past groups of his soldiers, Benedict offered praise and encouragement. But, he was becoming very concerned as he made his way onward. Many of the bateaus were falling apart. In a letter to Washington, Benedict wrote: "When you consider the badness and weight of the bateaus and large quantity of provisions, etc. we have been obliged to force up against a very rapid stream. You would have taken the men for amphibious animals, as they were a great part of time, underwater."

One of the first huge obstacles was Skowhegan Falls, a 100-foot drop in the river that Benedict described as "dangerous and difficult to pass." For those who have seen Skowhegan Falls, that would truly be an understatement. There, the river boils over enormous boulders.

Benedict managed to traverse some 50 miles in three days to catch up with Morgan's riflemen. They were trying to breach the next obstacle, Norridgewock Falls, a 90-foot drop of fast flowing rapids. It took the columns nearly a week to get up and around it. To this point, they had help from some of the local settlers, but the region farther west was pretty much wild and uncharted territory. Most of the columns, although exhausted, had made it past Norridgewock Falls by October 8, 1775.

As Benedict made the journey up river from this point, he described how "mountains began to appear on each side of the river, high and snow on tops." He had sent Morgan's riflemen on to the next obstacle, called the "Great Carrying Place." This was a 12-mile stretch of bogs, ponds, fallen trees and impassable brush. The weather also turned badly for the army. Torrential rains were followed by snow and bitter cold temperatures.

Slogging through, the men lost boats, cut their feet and hands while enduring rough, soggy terrain, cold and exhaustion. Some continued to drag bateaus along with them. Many became ill not only from hypothermia and fatigue, but also from drinking brackish water near the ponds. Benedict set up a makeshift hospital along the way. It was filled to capacity as soon as it was built. Supplies were running dangerously low because of so many losses in the river. Rations were supplemented with fish, the occasional moose and other wild game.

It took each of the four divisions a week to cross the Great Carrying Place and it took a huge toll, with so many sick and exhausted. There was much thought of turning back.

Portage of the Great Carrying Place. *Courtesy, Library of Congress.*

The Great Carrying Place took them to the Dead River, with miles more of streams and rapids. Their supplies were dwindling and Benedict reluctantly ordered half rations, hoping they could supplement with fish and wild game. Conditions worsened. Torrential rains fell from the 19th through the 22nd of October. The river rose some eight feet, forcing the men to look for higher ground. Everywhere they looked there was rushing, freezing cold water, to the point where it was impossible to make out any directions or trails.

The columns were now stretched out nearly 20 miles and much of their provisions were lost in the flood. Benedict had the men make a camp and called for a council of war with the officers in the area. They now realized they weren't in a race to win Quebec, but now a race to survive, with winter not far behind.

At the war council, Benedict gave his assessment first, but agreed to abide by the council's decision. He surmised there was no point in trying to retreat, as the danger of going back looked almost as difficult as pushing toward Canada and the nearest French settlement where provisions could be obtained. He also thought the men would soon reach Lake Megantic, where they wouldn't have to fight the currents. Benedict had no idea of the other prong of attack, as they were so isolated. He thought that if he could put together some fast teams, they could get to the French settlements and return with some supplies to stave off starvation.

Officers at the war council agreed to Benedict's plan, but everyone was definitely on edge. At this point, winter was setting in. Game and fish were almost impossible to find. They were facing starvation.

Unknown to Benedict, another council was convening at the far end of the column. Roger Enos, the head of the rear column, was truly suffering from what Dr. Senter called "faint heartedness." He took some of the sick and turned back to the Maine settlements with almost 300 troops, but without Benedict's permission. When news of the defection spread throughout the columns, many were disheartened, but pushed on. Enos also left with more than his share of the remaining provisions.

Enos and his division made it back to Cambridge. It was of note that Washington had him arrested and tried by court-martial. He was found not guilty, mainly because no one was there to speak against him. Benedict never showed any ill will or malice toward Enos because he knew what the men were enduring.

On October 25th, heavy snow and high winds hit the columns. Their next objective was Lake Megantic, but before they could get there, they had to cross the "Terrible Carrying Place." It was a steep two-mile march over the mountains dividing Maine and Canada. Some had to abandon what was left of their bateaus as they struggled through the snow and rocks. After successfully reaching the peak of the divide, they had another seven miles of log and rock-filled streams to descend before finally reaching the lake.

Benedict received a scouting report as they entered the seven-mile stream. Some scouts he had sent ahead reached a French settlement and said, "They appear very friendly and were rejoiced to hear of our approach." There were also no British forces to contend with in that area. It was the first good news in a very long time.

The column and divisions were now stretched out more than 20 miles. Provisions were all but gone. Many men were sick and delirious. They stumbled up and over the mountain pass, some dropping any unnecessary weight like tents and bateaus. Some even lost their weapons.

Jemima Warner, one of the women who had made the journey, lost her husband to exposure. No one had the strength or tools to bury him. She lingered with him for a bit before covering him with leaves. The grieving wife picked up her lost husband's rifle and caught up with the column. This brave, young American woman—probably only 19 to 21—was the first female to serve in American combat, proudly under the command of Benedict. She would later meet her end while manning an artillery battery during the Battle of Quebec. Surely, the daring Jemima qualified for induction to the Women's Hall of Fame at Seneca Falls, New York.

Mrs. Grier, another woman accompanying the troops into battle, was mentioned respectfully in letters written by some of the soldiers. Her fate is not known.

Desperate for any kind of food, men boiled candles and made gruel from hides or leather to be used for moccasins or boot repair. The starving soldiers ate lip salve and shaving soap. Captain Dearborn's Labrador dog—traveling with the troops—was eaten by the starving men. Dr. Senter wrote that the Labrador was taken by "assassinators" and "was instantly devoured, without leaving any vestige of the sacrifice." Other dogs also accompanied the march, but none lived to see the month of November.

Benedict knew the desperate situation his army was in and headed a fast team to reach the French settlements and bring back provisions for his men. While paddling up Lake Megantic, they found "a very considerable wigwam." It gave the men a place to dry out quickly and rest briefly from the harsh weather. The respite also gave Benedict a few moments to write a quick report for Washington. He penned: "I have been much deceived on every account of our route, which is longer and has been attended by a thousand difficulties I never apprehended. But if crowned with success, and conducive to the public good, I shall think it trifling."

Benedict pushed himself to the limit and soon reached the French settlement at Sartigan. He was welcomed warmly by the people there. They referred to his men as "Les Bostonnais." He bought whatever provisions the French could spare for his troops. He paid far more than the normal value, in the hope of bonding with the local population.

On the morning of November 2nd, the men couldn't believe their eyes. They saw cattle being headed toward them, followed by birch bark canoes loaded with grain, mutton and tobacco. One soldier wrote: "were blessed with the finest sight my eyes ever beheld." Another wrote that they "shed tears of joy in our happy delivery from the grasping hand of death."

Buoyed by nourishment, Benedict's men began moving the provisions toward the rear of the column as quickly as they could. It was too late for some. They looked for stragglers they could help, but some 40 or 50 brave young men had died of exposure and starvation.

Curiously, while the column traveled along the Dead River and toward Lake Megantic, they were passing through the Indian territory overseen by Chief Natanis. The Indians watched from a distance. Natanis was very impressed by Benedict, a leader who went to and fro, encouraging and helping his men. He even sent some of the braves out to dangerous places on the trail, to assist the soldiers. Natanis had never seen a leader of soldiers who showed so much compassion for his men. He was so impressed by Benedict that he would later follow him into the battle at the walls of Quebec.

The soldiers sifted in toward Sartigan. Benedict took a few good men—including Dr. Senter—and forged ahead, buying provisions and setting up food stations along the way to the St. Lawrence River. He got quite a few days ahead of the column and decided to go to a nearby settlement called the Village of Gilbert, where there was a large Native American community. Dr. Senter wrote that the tribe "addressed the colonel with great pomp."

Benedict parleyed with the tribe and must have made a persuasive argument as to why they should join and help the American army: "To drive out the king's soldiers." He must have made quite an impression, as Chief Natanis also spoke on his behalf. Forty of his warriors accepted a short-term enlistment in the army and agreed to help Benedict's comrades.

As Benedict's men regrouped and benefited from nourishment, morale began to rise again. Beside the bravery it took for Benedict to just walk in and parley with Native Americans, there was an interesting side story that attests to Benedict's character.

There was a Private "Henry" who was severely ill and sitting by the trail. Henry wrote: "The commander knew my name and character and good-naturedly inquired after my health." When Benedict saw how sick Henry was, he "ran down to the riverside and hailed the owner of the house which stood opposite across the water."

Benedict made arrangements for Henry's care, then handed the private two silver dollars so he could pay a French family for food and lodging while recovering there. It was one of many acts like this that endeared Benedict's men to him. Not exactly the self-serving interest portrayed in many history books.

It was early November 1775 when most of the forces reached the banks of the mighty St. Lawrence River. The number of men ready to attack Quebec was now down to 650. The weather had turned unusually cold and wet. Some officers obtained the use of horses, but one wrote that the horses were sinking nearly to their bellies on what were called roads.

Unfortunately, Benedict had lost the element of surprise. News had reached Quebec that a force was marching through Maine and the British forces in Quebec were preparing for an invasion.

On Sunday, November 5th, Benedict went to the local Roman Catholic church and presented it with Washington's proclamation of friendship. Benedict was hoping to enlist any assistance he could, but received none, as many were in fear of reprisal from British Governor Carlton. The governor had issued a message prior to Benedict's visit that "they were determined to burn and destroy all the inhabitants in the vicinity of Quebec unless they came in and took up arms in defense of the garrison."

Benedict also learned that the British forces in Canada were already engaging the American forces driving north from Albany.

CHAPTER NINE

Fight to Control the St. Lawrence & Quebec

The second prong of the American offensive into Canada—under the command of General Schuyler—traveled up Lake Champlain, where the general fell gravely ill. He was forced to retreat back to Albany. While recuperating there, he took charge of sending supplies north toward Canada. He also became sidetracked by negotiations with the Six Nations of the Iroquois Confederacy. Schuyler was attempting to keep the combined force of Native Americans neutral or to have them side with the Americans.

When Schuyler left the Champlain region, he left a very adept and experienced General Richard Montgomery in charge of the expedition. Montgomery was a former British officer and very experienced in warfare. He was hoping to position himself for glory in the American army. When he reached the north end of Lake Champlain, he first had to deal with the now reinforced fort of St. Johns. He spent 45 days laying siege. It took until

November 2nd of 1775, but he brought about the surrender of 700 British regulars and Canadian defenders.

It is interesting to note that one of the captured prisoners of war who survived the siege at St. Johns was a young British officer named John Andre'. More was to be heard about him.

Governor and Commander Guy Carlton—in charge of the British forces in Canada—was in a bit of a pickle. He had already been embarrassed by losing the Champlain region to this "horse jockey," Benedict Arnold. Now, he had a threat reaching toward the St. Lawrence and Quebec. He heard rumors and had intelligence about Benedict's forces coming through Maine, but he had to deal with Montgomery's siege of St. Johns.

Carlton left Quebec quite lightly defended and put out desperate calls to England for reinforcements to hold the region. He sailed down river to Montreal, to try and bolster support for defense of the city, but was largely unsuccessful in gaining Canadian assistance. Carlton had some highly trained, veteran troops with him, under the command of Colonel Allan Maclean. A division of about 170 Royal Highland Emigrants was commanded by Maclean.

Maclean was ordered by Carlton to sail back to Quebec to help defend the city. As Maclean faced a strong headwind and wasn't making much progress downriver,

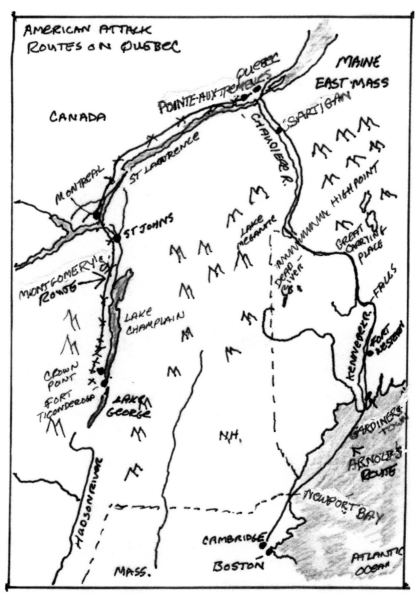

American Attack on Quebec

he captured two Indians who were acting as couriers for Benedict. They carried information of Benedict's force near Quebec. Maclean knew he had to get back quickly to defend Quebec City. He abandoned the ship and his men marched overland back to the walled city, arriving there on November 12th.

It was the same day Benedict was holding a council of war to discuss with his men the taking of Quebec. Had Maclean not intercepted Benedict's couriers, the Americans might have taken the largely undefended City of Quebec and controlled the St. Lawrence.

Benedict's men could see their goal, the walled City of Quebec, on the far side of the St. Lawrence River. The high, ten-feet thick stone walls that encircled most of city loomed over the river. Two British warships were anchored near her port. Benedict constantly sent out reconnaissance to ascertain the city's defensive strength and to find out where Montgomery was.

During the November 12th council of war, it was decided that if the wind subsided, a night crossing would be attempted and be, hopefully, undetected. If all went well, maybe even a preemptive strike would be tried. The British had already destroyed most of the boats in the area, just to thwart such an attempt. But Benedict's men had gathered a small armada of bateaus and canoes in preparation.

Later the following night, the winds faded away and the crossing was launched. It took four waves of men to get most of the force across. By 4 a.m. of the next morning, 500 men had crossed the great river silently and undetected. During the night crossing, one of the canoes capsized, throwing its men into the freezing waters of the St. Lawrence. With the help of their comrades, the men were fished out of the water and taken to the shore. There, they found a small hut and started a fire to keep from freezing to death.

A group of British seamen saw the glow of the fire in the hut and rowed a small boat to the site to investigate. Shots rang out and three of the British seamen were hit with musket fire. Benedict's men then knew the element of surprise was slipping away. They decided an assault on the city was out of the question. Some houses outside the walls were seized and Benedict had the chance to rest his men under the watch of guards he posted there.

As the next few days passed, Benedict and Maclean were busy gathering intelligence about the strength of arms held by each. Some civilians were fleeing the city, while others were going to the city for protection. To obtain information, both armies questioned those coming and going.

On November 14th of 1775, Benedict decided to try a show of force. He spread his men out in the fields in front of the city, known as the "Plains of Abraham." They offered huzzahs and rifle fire in the name of liberty. The British responded with cannon fire. It was all pretty much for show because of the distance involved.

Benedict then sent some of his men under a white flag with terms of surrender, but they were fired on and that infuriated Benedict. His little army had only five rounds of ammunition per soldier and certainly not enough men to storm such a well-fortified city by themselves. They decided reluctantly to pull back and wait for reinforcements from Montgomery.

In colonial times, the only form of communication was letters and couriers were constantly moving under orders to relay messages. There were also many trying to intercept these brave messengers to gain their treasured information. It was a very dangerous job. One of the couriers used in Canada was well known—the feisty little Aaron Burr.

Benedict was not the type to take retreating or waiting very well. He penned a letter to Washington, saying, "If only I had been ten days sooner, Quebec would have fallen into our hands." He added that he was waiting with "great anxiety" for General Montgomery's help.

The curious and odd thing that Benedict didn't know was that Carlton, the governor and commander of Canada and Quebec, was trapped between Montgomery

The Philadelphia II, replica of the 1776 gunboat. *Courtesy, Lake Champlain Maritime Museum.*

and Benedict. He had tried to get back quickly to Quebec, but the winds held him on the river and his fleet was under fire from American cannons on the shore.

The Americans demanded surrender of the British ship with Carlton on board. He refused to be captured and disguised himself as an inhabitant of Canada, complete with a wool cap. He was lowered off the warship and into a whaling boat in the middle of the night. The men in the whaling boat paddled silently with their hands and slipped through the American blockade of the river. By dawn, they had passed the blockade and were picked up by a British boat. Carlton made it safely past Benedict, who had seen the ship, but had no idea Carlton was on board.

By November 19th, Carlton made it back to the walls of Quebec. It was the same day Benedict was setting up camp in a small French village called Pointe-Aux-Trembles. Its citizens greeted Benedict warmly and gladly provided the troops with what they needed, including leather to make boots, as most had been eaten or destroyed by the terrain during the march through Maine.

Benedict paid dearly out of his own funds to meet his troops' needs and extended his credit with local merchants. Some of the merchants were trading partners with Benedict before the war.

Montgomery also had his hands full. He had just taken Montreal on November 13th and was overseeing security there. Benedict penned a letter to him, stating his need for more supplies, provisions and hard cash, as his were "nearly exhausted." He knew merchants he had traded with in Montreal "that might be able to help or lend credit." He related that too much had already been borne by his Kennebec column.

Troops and supplies were gathered by Montgomery in the hope of reinforcing Benedict. He left his second-in-command, General David Wooster of Connecticut, in charge of garrisoning Montreal with about 500 troops. Wooster was an older member of the elite class and he was upset with the Continental Congress for only giving him a brigadier's commission. He also resented serving under Montgomery.

General Montgomery finally came into view of Benedict's position on December 1st, 1775. He traveled up the St. Lawrence River with a contingent of 1,325 soldiers, most from New York. The number was almost 700 short of what Benedict had requested and believed would be necessary to storm Quebec.

A painting by F. C. Yohn depicts the storming of Quebec in blinding snow. Benedict was the first man in, and the first man shot. For many, it was their last day of enlistment, and their last day on earth. *Courtesy, Library of Congress.*

CHAPTER TEN

Storming Quebec: Liberty or Death

Montgomery and Benedict began planning together on the first day of December 1775. Montgomery had a wealth of military experience and was well schooled in British tactics. He suggested they had three options: siege, investment or storm. Time and weather ruled out siege or investment. They knew the British would be sending reinforcements as soon as they could. If Quebec didn't fall before their arrival, all efforts would be in vain.

Quebec was also growing in strength daily. In November, some 150 more Royal Highland Emigrants arrived from Newfoundland, along with a supply ship from England. Carlton would also draft the inhabitants of the city to take up arms.

Storming the city was the only viable option. It was decided they would start by harassing and wearing down the defenders from the outside. The plan was to not let them rest and keep them guessing when an assault would come.

Benedict pointed out that any assault needed to be launched by the first day of January, since many of the soldiers' enlistments would be ended by then. He knew the men were eager to go home, and considering what they had been through, he couldn't blame them.

In a letter Montgomery penned back to General Schuyler, there was telling information about Benedict and his column. He wrote of Colonel Arnold's detachment: That they were an "exceedingly fine one," certainly "injured by fatigue." But there is a "style of discipline" among his troops, "much superior to what I have been used to seeing in this campaign." Regarding Benedict, he said he was "active, intelligent and enterprising." Montgomery said he was paying "particular attention to Colonel Arnold's recommendations."

Montgomery brought with him cannons he had seized from Fort St. Johns. A campaign of harassment was begun through the month of December. Artillery batteries were formed out of ice, since digging in the frozen ground was impossible. This was where the first woman killed in American combat met her fate. Jemima Warner's artillery position was hit by cannon fire from the wall around Quebec.

Daniel Morgan's riflemen were put to good use as snipers. Under the cover of homes outside the city, these excellent marksmen picked sentries off the city's protective walls. By passing letters into the city, attempts were made to persuade the civilian population to put pressure on or resort to mutiny against the British rulers.

At night, they moved artillery batteries closer to the walled city in order to be more effective, but they were so outgunned by the heavier artillery of the British that they received much more damage than they delivered. One soldier wrote that his artillery was like "peas hitting a plank."

On December 15th, Benedict, one of the captains and a drummer marched up to the city gates under a flag of truce and demanded to speak with Governor Carlton. Benedict carried a letter offering safe passage to England for the British officers, if they should choose the wise course of surrender.

In the frigid air, Carlton made them wait for a reply, then sent the message that he would never negotiate with rebel scum. As Benedict left, he shouted, "Then let the general be answerable for all consequences."

Carlton knew if he could hold his position behind the heavily fortified city, relief would come from England when the weather broke. He also knew the extreme cold and heavy snow had to be wearing down the rebel force. And he was correct. Many suffered frostbite, there were desertions and numerous Americans were reaching the end of their enlistments and dreaming of going home.

The plan of harassment was largely ineffective. The men were instructed to build scaling ladders to mount the walls when the opportunity presented itself. The officers formed a plan of attack from two different directions, to confuse the enemy and, hopefully, force a surrender. The signal for the attack to begin would be rocket fire and the appointed time would be under the cover of darkness at 4:30 a.m.

Benedict's troops were instructed to wear sprigs of hemlock and a piece of paper on their hats so they could tell friend from foe, once inside the city walls. All of the hat papers were marked with the same three words: "Liberty or Death."

In a howling snowstorm on December 31st of 1775, all men were positioned by 4 a.m. It was the last day of their enlistment period and many felt it would be their last day on earth. Most commanders of the era thought it more prudent to direct their forces from a distance, but Benedict had a working class mindset. He never asked anyone to do something he wasn't willing to do himself.

When the rocket signal went off, Benedict led his column along the narrow pathway toward the first barricade of the city. Heavy snow was biting his face and he could hear the city's warning bells ringing. He was the first man to confront British musket fire.

Benedict sustained a horrible shot to his lower left leg. He fell into the snow, but urged the force forward and on to victory as he lay on the ground.

As Daniel Morgan caught up with his friend and commander, he could see that Benedict was bleeding from his boot. He directed that Benedict be carried to a general hospital set up for the wounded. The hospital was located in a home about a mile from the city.

Morgan then pressed his men forward. Besides Benedict, Morgan was probably the hardiest and fiercest fighter most have ever read about. Morgan and his men made it past the first barrier but lost many to wounds and death. He yelled for the scaling ladders to be positioned for going over the huge wall surrounding Quebec.

As Morgan led the charge over the wall, a volley of enemy musket fire threw him backward and he landed in the snow. Men began to panic in the fear that their leader, Daniel Morgan, was dead. But he was just knocked out, with his face blackened and bleeding from gunpowder burns.

When Morgan regained consciousness, he shouted to his men to follow him and he charged back up the ladder. He vaulted over the wall, landing on a platform that held two cannons. Somehow, he managed to land between the barrels of the cannons. His men quickly followed and the surprised British forces retreated in panic.

Before assaulting the next barrier, Morgan was hoping to hear Montgomery's division charging from the other side, but it was all too quiet. A British captain swung open the barricade and demanded that Morgan's men lay down their arms. Morgan shot the man dead on the spot and his troops surged forward and into a horrible volley of musket fire that stopped their advance.

Carlton sent men from different directions, ferociously firing on the patriot army. Shots were also raining down on them from the top of the wall. Some took cover in shops along the street, but the attack was ending by 10 a.m.

Morgan was one of the last to surrender. He was cornered against a wall and surrounded, but said he would not give up his sword to a tyrannical British government. He slashed his sword at anyone daring to get close. Finally, a priest appeared and offered to accept his sword so Morgan could surrender with honor.

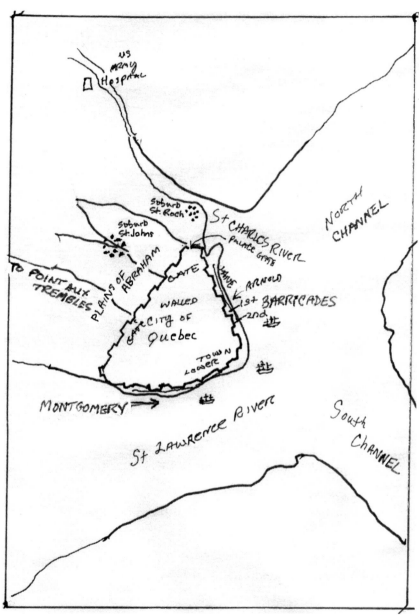

Assault on Quebec City

Montgomery's prong of attack from the upper part of the city made it past the first barrier. General Montgomery raised his sword to direct the men toward the second barrier, where unknown to them, were mounted cannons and musket men hidden in a log structure at point blank range.

When Montgomery raised his sword, he died instantly. His men offered some resistance at the fortified structure, but because of the snow and wind, many muskets wouldn't fire. The troops panicked and fled back to the Plains of Abraham. Benedict, not being able to put weight on his leg, was carried to the field hospital that was under the command of Dr. Senter, his friend who marched with him through Maine. Dr. Senter later wrote of Benedict's wounds: "The ball had entered the outside of the leg, midway between the knee and ankle, then took an oblique course downward and lodged in the rise of the Achilles."

Dr. Senter probed for the ball and easily extracted it. Once the bleeding was under control, the doctor bandaged the wound and informed Benedict that amputation wouldn't be needed unless infection set in.

As more wounded poured into the hospital, Benedict kept gathering the sad news of how the attack was progressing. His heart sank when he learned of Montgomery's death, and worse, the surrender of his Kennebec warriors and Daniel Morgan.

In his zeal of overcoming the patriot attack, Carlton sent a division toward the hospital to crush the remaining rebels. Suddenly, a breathless artillery Captain Wool burst into the hospital and told Benedict about an advancing force. Benedict asked him to offer resistance if he could. Wool called on anyone who could still fight, wounded or not, to join him in the street.

Two cannons were dragged toward Quebec and hidden among the trees. When the British division was in range, a mighty round of fire was aimed at them. The surprised soldiers retreated. The hospital and remaining soldiers were spared.

Dr. Senter pleaded with Benedict, for his own safety, that he be carried back further into the countryside so the enemy would not find him. Benedict steadfastly refused. He ordered that his pistols be loaded and his sword placed on his bed. He also ordered a loaded weapon for every wounded soldier. Benedict said he was "determined to kill as many as possible if they came into the room."

As he lay there in agonizing pain, Benedict penned a letter to the remaining forces in Montreal, informing them of their "critical situation" and the urgent need for reinforcement. As he sent the courier to Montreal, he made it clear that there would be no notion of retreat until he knew the fate of his men. The following day, Carlton sent an envoy with one of his prisoners, a Captain Meigs, asking for any personal effects and baggage for the care of his prisoners of war.

With a heavy heart, Benedict now knew the fate of his men. Patriot losses stood at 51 killed, 36 wounded and nearly two thirds of his column captured as prisoners. Benedict had as many personal effects gathered as he could to send back with the envoy and Captain Meigs. He also gave money from his own pocket to help provide good care for his comrades.

It was not the beginning of a happy new year for 1776.

CHAPTER ELEVEN

The Start of 1776 & the Longest Cold Winter

Benedict steadfastly refused to retreat and he eventually had himself moved to larger quarters, bedridden with his leg wound. Due to the intense pain, he decided to turn over his outside duties to one of his captains. Although he couldn't get outside, he could write letters and send couriers to try and improve a very bad situation.

Many of the remaining men reached the end of their enlistments and some left camp to go home. Benedict, being confined to bed rest, could do nothing to bolster their support or get them to re-enlist.

To make matters worse, all of his supplies were running dangerously low and Benedict also needed cash to pay for Canadian assistance. Many of the Canadians were on the side of American liberty, but Benedict feared that if money ran out, so would much of their support.

The winter outside was howling. It was one of worst winters in Canadian history. Benedict had a siege he wanted desperately to maintain and he hoped that if he could get reinforcements, he would launch a second assault to try and free his comrades. He was also short of gunpowder and due to the winter conditions, only two of every ten muskets could fire properly.

Luckily, British Governor Carlton remained in his defensive position inside the walls of Quebec. Had he decided to attack, the small American army would have easily been over-run. But Benedict and Carlton knew as winter ended and the ice on the mighty St. Lawrence began to break up, Great Britain would be bearing down with force to retake what the Americans had gained.

From his bed, Benedict sent couriers out into the icy, windy winter landscape at a blinding pace. Letters went out in every direction. He wrote first to General Wooster, an older aristocratic general from Connecticut, who Montgomery left in charge of Montreal after his departure. With General Montgomery's death in battle, General Wooster became the main commander in the region.

Wooster immediately sent out 150 men and supplies to relieve Benedict, but he made no serious effort to leave Montreal himself. Benedict then wrote to General Schuyler, Washington and Congress about his grave situation. He pleaded for more troops and supplies. He also had feelings of inadequacy. One January 11th letter asked the delegates of Congress to send "an experienced General... as early as possible."

Unknown to Benedict was his growing hero status in the colonies. Thomas Jefferson was comparing him to Hannibal going over the Alps or Xenophon's retreat in classic warfare. He also suggested that Benedict should receive the fallen Montgomery's major generalship. Samuel Adams was one of his biggest supporters, referring to Benedict as a "genius." Adams did all he could to try and revive the campaign before Britain could reinforce Quebec.

General Schuyler also sang Benedict's praises and called for many efforts to reinforce him. Benedict Arnold, in the 1775 campaign season—with a handful of men—accomplished more than Washington had with thousands. Washington was more than a little jealous and fearful of Benedict's growing popularity. All this time, he was still encamped around Boston. Congress petitioned him to release some of his men for a relief effort.

But Washington wrote, "I have not a man to spare," although he boasted about Benedict's efforts in the northern campaign, since he was under Washington's command. He may have started seeing the second-class colonel as a threat to his glory.

In March of 1776, Washington finally captured Dorchester Heights, placing fortifications and cannons that threatened the harbored British fleet. The cannon placement, being in range of British ships, forced the British fleet to leave Boston. But as much glory as George Washington received from chasing the Redcoats out of Boston, everyone knew the cannons used to accomplish it came from Benedict's adventures in the Champlain region.

Benedict's name was spreading as far as London. It was beyond belief that this horse trader from Connecticut—lacking proper breeding—was becoming a force to be reckoned with.

By the end of January 1776, as winter howled in Quebec, Benedict's leg began to slowly heal. He felt like a caged animal. He began hobbling around, against Dr. Senter's orders, and he decided to resume his full duties. His distress calls were slowly being answered. Benedict was welcoming troops, as they slowly poured into camp through blinding blizzard conditions.

Benedict's hope of a second assault began to rise, as his troop numbers were up to 2,505 by the end of March. Now, one of the biggest threats to his small army was an outbreak of small pox. Up to a third of the men "were unfit for duty." Many were horribly sick, with some at death's door. A makeshift hospital was set up to quarantine the cases as they appeared, but by the end of March, Dr. Senter was out of medicine. Small pox ran rampantly through the camp and also within the walls of Quebec.

Benedict forbade the practice of self-inoculation, but many soldiers went through with it. They sliced themselves open—usually in the thigh area—then took active, infectious pustules from a small pox victim and placed them in the wound. The disease would still be contracted, but it wouldn't be as severe. This practice would render a man useless for nearly three or four weeks.

Also suffered were colds, pneumonia and frostbite that caused the loss of fingers and toes. Just surviving the winter of early '76 was a battle within itself. Benedict made note at the end of March of nearly five feet of remaining snow "sufficiently hard to bear a man and horse."

Small pox was raging within the walls of Quebec. Although there were ample food stores, there was a desperate need for firewood. A British military detachment was sent out to gather wood, and on one occasion, they left the city in force. They brought with them rolling brass cannons to protect the men while they gathered every bit of wood they could find, including boards from houses and fences. In a short time, they rushed back to the city with nearly 40 cords of wood, before the rebel army could react.

By March, Benedict began planning a second assault on the city. He also started a harsh campaign of harassment. He was hoping to get the civilian population to revolt or at least force Carlton's troops into open combat. He slowly burned down most of the city's surrounding suburbs, trying to force Carlton's hand, but to no effect. Carlton stubbornly stayed behind the high wall defenses.

Benedict also wanted to destroy British warships moored in Quebec's harbor. As part of his battle plan, he decided to make use of his own merchant ship, the "Peggy." She was moored in the area with a cargo of rum. The Peggy, which was named for Benedict's wife, represented a third of Benedict's personal source of income. It must have pained him terribly, but he felt the sacrifice was justified in the cause of liberty.

The cargo of rum was unloaded, "which the men appreciated," and the ship's hull was filled with explosives. Benedict's idea was to sail her into the British warships and blow her up to cause their destruction. This surely wasn't the act of a self-serving patriot, as many history books have reported.

Benedict received a message informing him he had been promoted to Brigadier General by Congress. This lifted his spirits as he hurried to make preparations for a second assault on Quebec. But with such little military experience, he still felt inadequate for the mission and kept requesting a ranking general for the area. Everyone knew time was running out for any attempt to take the city. By late March, the ice on the St. Lawrence was beginning to break up and reinforcements from Britain were surely on their way.

On April 1st of 1776, David Wooster, the commanding general in the area, finally moved from his comfortable quarters in Montreal to Quebec. The next morning, Benedict gave him a tour by horseback of all the patriot positions he had been working on and details of his preparations. Wooster grumbled about everything he saw and after the tour he dismissed any advice or recommendations Benedict had offered.

Benedict was trying very hard to suppress his anger and frustration with Wooster, especially with all they had endured over the past three months. That very day, sudden word came that Carlton was planning a foray out of the city. Benedict, ready for action, ran to his horse. The mount suddenly spooked and reared, causing Benedict to lose his balance. His horse crashed to the ground, pinning Benedict's wounded leg.

Carried back into his headquarters, Benedict was again bedridden for another ten days. It was like darkness had fallen over him and the camp. Carlton's move turned out to be a false alarm. Benedict knew he probably couldn't hold back his anger with Wooster much longer. He requested permission to retire back to Montreal. Wooster considered Benedict a second-class, inexperienced, overzealous soldier and easily granted his request.

On April 12th of 1776, a very dejected Benedict rode out of Quebec to Montreal. He was very slowly learning a new reality. In the business world, as long as he had the freedom—which he was willing to fight for—he could always set his own destiny. All he needed was his own strength, merit and skills in order to succeed or fail.

But in colonial America, there was a new world of rank, politics and class for Benedict to adjust to, and his perseverance was not always enough. He found others could undermine his efforts, actions and honor. This, to Benedict, was a very bitter pill to swallow.

As Benedict rode into Montreal, he was in search of General Wooster's former headquarters. He found out Wooster spent a very comfortable winter at a chateau on the river. Benedict assumed command of the city and began receiving meetings with prominent residents. Some of them were old trading acquaintances of Benedict's.

Benedict heard many complaints of Wooster's high-handedness throughout the winter. He assured the residents he would do his best to make amends. He had little time to rest or reflect on his quest in Quebec and the harsh winter of 1775. There were rumors of preparation in progress for an assault on Montreal, from the west. The British in the outposts of the wilderness regions along Lake Ontario had aligned with some Native Americans and were hoping to attack rebel forces around Montreal.

Available troops under Benedict's command had to prepare for a possible assault, and if Wooster failed in Quebec, he needed to prepare for an orderly retreat toward the Champlain corridor. Washington was busy moving his main army toward New York City, as he felt Britain's next move would be targeted there. Apprehension and fear were beginning to build in the Montreal area, knowing Great Britain's ships and reinforcements could arrive any day to retake the region.

Benedict received a surprise visit at headquarters on April 26th, 1776. Congress had sent a new commander, Major General John Thomas, to the Quebec region. Thomas was a doctor by trade, but he had much military experience in the Seven Years War in Canada. He was 51 and described as very tall.

Thomas was anxious to meet Benedict Arnold, who was growing in fame. Thomas had heard much about Benedict. He told Benedict he was being referred to as "America's Hannibal" in the halls of Congress and brought warm greetings from Washington. He also needed to get Benedict's opinions on the Canadian affairs.

Benedict relayed the sad state the Canadian campaign was in, not pulling any punches. They talked for hours of possible ways to reinvigorate efforts before the British arrived. Thomas told Benedict he had close to 1,500 patriot soldiers at Fort Ticonderoga and Crown Point, waiting for the ice clogged waterways to open so they could move north to help. Thomas also informed Benedict that a small envoy of congressional commissioners from Philadelphia would be along in a few days to see him and assess the situation.

He was hoping they were bringing some hard money, said Benedict, to reimburse the Canadians who had sacrificed so many goods to maintain the army. Thomas told him maybe they could help with the politics, but he thought all they would be bringing was good will.

General Thomas moved on to Quebec to see how Wooster was handling affairs there. On April 29, 1776, the Philadelphia commissioners arrived. Benedict received them with "great pomp and a salute of cannons." The citizens of Montreal turned out to see what all the fuss was about. The head of the delegation was none other than Ben Franklin. At 70 years of age, the journey from Pennsylvania to Canada must have been arduous for him.

Franklin's mission was three-fold. He wanted to assess conditions in the northern theater for himself and he also wanted to meet and bolster support from the Canadian population, hoping to get them to join in the struggle, as a 14th colony. Not the least, Franklin was curious to meet Benedict Arnold, who had accomplished so much, given so little. Franklin was very much impressed by Benedict. He remained a friend and strong supporter of him throughout the war.

The other men in the delegation were Samuel Chase and Charles Carroll of Maryland. Both were delegates to the First and Second Continental Congresses. Carroll spoke fluent French and brought along Father John Carroll, a cousin who was a Jesuit priest. They would prove to be a great asset in dealing with the French Canadian Catholic population and leadership.

Benedict assessed the situation for the delegates and impressed on them the need for currency, to maintain Canadian support and to settle accounts owed. If they were to continue the Canadian campaign, he stated, he wanted to do it "with honor." The delegation wrote back to Congress for the need of close to 20,000 pounds, to "regain the affections of the people," and if funds weren't available, it would be "better immediately to withdraw."

By the end of May, all the decisions in the region were

made for the patriot force. They received news of a sizable British relief force that had crossed the Atlantic and was bearing down on them. Benedict asked the commission for permission to head back to Quebec to do "everything in his power to keep possession of this country." The commission agreed, but cautioned Benedict not to make too bold a stand, if forces were too great to repel. They might need to fall back to save patriot soldiers and fight another day.

Ben Franklin started making his way back to Philadelphia, but Carroll and Chase stayed behind to bolster Canadian support. Congress instructed Washington to detach troops, and he finally sent 2,000 men, but it was too little, too late. By the time the troops made it to the Richelieu River—at the northern part of the Champlain corridor—the American army was already in full retreat.

Benedict met up with General Thomas, who was already retreating from Quebec. He updated Benedict on the situation there. Thomas tried to implement some of Benedict's battle plans, but was to meet with much resistance from Wooster and other officers. He told Benedict that they did sail his merchant ship, Peggy, into the harbor with her now deadly cargo. But the British warships blew her up before she could do the intended damage.

The generous sacrifice of Benedict's ship and cargo was for naught. His men were on reduced rations and close to half had contracted small pox. Orderly retreat was their only option left.

On his way back toward Montreal, Benedict was met with more bad news. A British Commander "Forster" had made allies with the Conasadaga Indians and was making a move from the southwest toward Montreal. Forster engaged Benedict's troops at Fort Anne, a small fort to the west. He managed to capture 500 patriots, killing 28 of them. The Indians stripped the men of all their possessions, even some of their clothes.

Benedict was infuriated and began preparing to attack this force. He had no intentions of leaving more prisoners behind in Canada. Benedict gathered as many men fit for duty as he could find—about 450—and made a rush toward Forster's position.

Forster had received false reports that Benedict was advancing toward him with more men than Benedict actually had, and heard others were joining him. He decided to retreat west with his prisoners in tow.

Benedict reached Fort Anne, where the men were overrun and captured. He could see the retreating force in the distance. He sent a party of Caughnawaga (Indians allied with the patriots) ahead with a message. He wrote: "Should his men not be freed, or if any of them were murdered," he intended "to sacrifice every Indian that fell into my hands and would follow them to their towns and destroy them by fire and sword."

Forster wrote back a reply, saying, "If Arnold followed, he would kill every prisoner and give no quarter to any that fell into my hands." Benedict was furious at his reply and loaded 300 men into bateaus they found still intact at Fort Anne. They gave chase and received enemy fire at dusk, then silently rowed past the enemy position to cut off their escape route.

That night, Forster sent two prisoners with a truce flag to Benedict to suggest a prisoner exchange. Benedict's captains voted against any attack, as they were so outnumbered. Benedict decided to try to bluff Forster, since he knew Forster didn't know how many men Benedict had. He wrote back to Forster to say he was ready to launch an attack and "If our prisoners were murdered, his force would sacrifice every soul that fell in our hands."

Forster took the bait since he had his own problems and wasn't sure whether he could control the actions of his Indians, who were eager to kill and scalp the prisoners. The next day, he began to ferry the prisoners back to Fort Anne.

After securing the men back, Benedict left his officers in charge of moving them south toward Lake Champlain. He gave orders to burn Fort Anne and the Indian village along the way. He then hurried back to Montreal to help with the evacuation. Benedict's men decided not to burn the Indian village, due to rumors and scouting reports of strong Indian resistance.

Chase and Carroll were still in Montreal and were much relieved to hear the soldiers captured at Fort Anne were safe. The commissioners now knew of the impending, looming threat traveling down the St. Lawrence. They also knew of the bad condition of the retreating army and judged the Canadian campaign beyond repair. Before they left for Philadelphia, they wrote a letter to Congress, stating that General Thomas was dying of small pox and they wrote of Wooster's actions in the theater, saying he was totally unfit for command, thus he should be recalled immediately.

Benedict was asked by Chase and Carroll to assume overall command until another senior officer could take over. They begged for a load of supplies from the good citizens of Montreal, pledging payment at a later date, on the "Faith of the united colonies."

On May 31st of 1776, Benedict wrote a letter to General Gates, informing him of the mission. He was very downhearted, especially not wanting to leave his troops who were imprisoned in Quebec. But he knew, for now, there was no choice. He wrote that the group was "neglected by Congress" and had never received envoys and timely support. Benedict would use all his strength "making every possible preparation to secure and retreat"—which he was hoping to do with honor.

Benedict also wrote with frustration, "I wish with all my heart we were out of the country. We had much better begin anew and set out right and methodically."

The very day that letter was sent, a new commanding general was sent to the area by Washington for relief efforts and hopes of somehow turning events around. His name was General John Sullivan, a lawyer from New Hampshire and a delegate to the Continental Congress. He—like Benedict—had lots of zeal, but little military experience.

Sullivan ignored Benedict's advice and gathered any troops who were still in condition to fight. He decided to make a stand and engage the now-reinforced British troops between Montreal and Quebec. Sullivan was badly routed out, with 400 patriot losses, half of them imprisoned.

Benedict galloped at a feverish pace between Montreal and St. Johns, attending to evacuation details. He had a makeshift hospital set up on an island, the "Isle Aux Noix." It was 12 miles up the Richelieu River toward Lake Champlain. Benedict needed a place to safely care for the very sick and disease-ridden troops, as they made their way south.

On June 13th, he wrote to General Schuyler for the need of any kind of watercraft available to move men back down Lake Champlain. He stated, "You may expect soon to hear of evacuating Canada, or being prisoners."

General Sullivan arrived at St. Johns with what was left of his rear guard on June 17th. His troops had set fire to any forts they passed along the way. They gathered as many boats and canoes as they could find and destroyed as many bridges as they could, to slow the advance of the British troops who were not far behind.

On June 18th, Benedict ordered his remaining men into the boats and told them to go. He and an aide rode by horseback north to see how far behind them the British troops were. They rode hard north until they met up with General John Burgoyne's advance columns. He needed to know how much time they had.

Then, they rode quickly back to the shoreline, where they hurriedly unsaddled and unbridled their horses. Benedict pulled his pistol and shot his horse, telling his aide to do the same. They could leave nothing for the enemy to find and use against them. Benedict pushed the last boat from the Canadian shores by himself.

They arrived at the makeshift hospital on the Isle Aux Noix that very evening. The island was a horrible site of unspeakable distress. The sick—some of who could not see, speak or walk—were enduring maggots that crawled over their smallpox-ravaged bodies. Those healthy enough to continue were dragging their dead comrades into shallow burial pits.

A very heavyhearted Benedict had to turn his attention to the thousands of British troops poised to march on northern New York. Intelligence reports said there were well over 8,000 well-trained and well-supplied British troops preparing to advance. He found General Sullivan, who was also on the island.

Sullivan asked Benedict to take a letter describing the situation to General Schuyler, who was probably between Fort Ticonderoga and Albany. Benedict was more than happy to comply with Sullivan's request, just to get off the island of misery. He set off with Sullivan's letter immediately and finally got some rest as he sailed down Lake Champlain. It was the first rest he had gotten in many days.

Schuyler wasn't at Fort Ticonderoga, so Benedict went south to Albany, where he caught up with Schuyler on June 24th of 1776. Benedict was anxious to discuss defending the Champlain corridor. Both armies were now locked in a race to build offensive and defensive capabilities, in order to travel the length of Champlain.

CHAPTER TWELVE

The Battle for Canada Ends & the Battle for Survival of the Colonies Begins

For those who think our forefathers were all gentlemen working in harmony, that was not the case. The political wrangling, backbiting and debauchery were outrageous, and in 1776 were reaching a feverish pace. It seems when there was a victory of any kind, there were many ready and willing to claim credit, even discrediting others to do so.

But when word of the lost Canadian campaign hit Congress, the blame game hit an all time high. There were courts of inquiry, accusations from junior officers who felt compelled to testify and many character assassinations. Benedict considered them small-minded, self-serving patriots and many of them were.

General Schuyler was hit with many accusations, even to the level of treason. Sullivan, Benedict, Wooster and Thomas all came under fire. Washington made sure he didn't catch any blame and suggested sending General

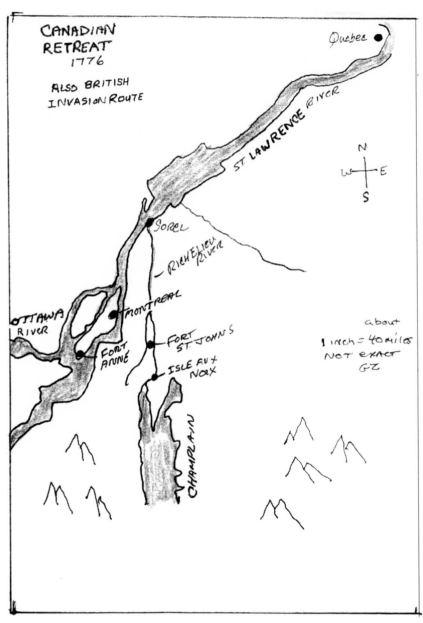

Canadian Retreat, 1776

Horatio Gates to take control of the northern theater. Schuyler saw this move as a threat to his command and leadership. But he managed to defend himself quite well in Congress and cleared his name.

Schuyler now had Gates to deal with. Benedict, for his part, was just busy trying to get the job done. He thought it best to let his actions speak for themselves. Men like Schuyler, Washington and Gates—of the upper class—knew this political maneuvering would be more important later on and paid more particular attention to it.

When Gates arrived in Albany, he, Benedict and Schuyler left together to get back to the Champlain region. They arrived at Crown Point on July 5th of 1776. The northern army, what was left of it, had to regroup. The long Canadian campaign had taken a terrible toll. A total of 5,000 men went north. Many were wounded and recovering. Many with small pox were too sick to fight, some were missing in action and a good number were prisoners of war.

At the north end of Lake Champlain was the huge reinforced British army preparing to bear down on the patriots. General Sullivan became very upset over being replaced with Gates and felt he had to go to Philadelphia to defend his honor. There was also much tension between Gates and Schuyler, as now there were two commanding generals in the same theater.

General Philip Schuyler, Commander of the northern
army, negotiator with the Iroquois, and supporter of
Arnold. Schuyler survived accusation of treason by
Washington. *Courtesy, Library of Congress.*

On July 7th of 1776, Schuyler called for a council of
war. He agreed to leave the main command in Gates'
hands when he wasn't in the theater. The main points
of defense on the lake were Fort Crown Point and
Old Fort Ticonderoga. It was clear that there weren't
enough resources to defend both forts. Fort Ticonderoga was chosen, but Benedict pointed out that the
old fort was nearby Mount Defiance. If the British
maneuvered cannons to her summit, they could easily

rain artillery into the fort. Many at the council scoffed, saying cannons could never be hauled up such steep and wooded terrain.

After the war council, Sullivan left for Philadelphia to offer his resignation and defend his honor. General Schuyler also left the area, as he had an urgent matter to attend to. He was in the middle of negotiations with the Iroquois Nation. He was hoping to gain their neutrality. The Iroquois could easily upset any supply lines and communications if they took the side of Great Britain.

Schuyler was largely successful with all the tribes, except the fiercest—the Mohawks and Senecas. Most of the other tribes agreed to stay neutral or side with the Americans.

By late July, the American troops received the news that Congress had issued a formal "Declaration of Independence." It gave the men a more definite idea of what they were fighting for and morale started to lift in the camp.

But storm clouds were surely forming on the horizon. In June and July, a massive British war fleet arrived at New York's harbor. Some 30 battleships armed with 1,200 cannons, 30,000 soldiers and 10,000 sailors were accompanied by 300 supply ships. The British fleet was under the command of General William Howe and his brother, Admiral Lord Richard Howe.

The new, young America was about to be crushed and the rebellion put down.

With the incredible British force in New York City under Howe and another huge force in Canada under Governor Carlton and General Burgoyne, the situation for the small American army looked quite bleak. The campaign season was running toward fall and the American army needed to find a way to slow the British advance or face a crushing defeat before winter.

CHAPTER THIRTEEN

Commodore Benedict Arnold— Father of the American Navy

At Fort Ticonderoga, General Gates began formulating his defensive battle plans. The obvious way for Carlton and Burgoyne to attack south was to go down Lake Champlain. Gates needed a way to slow the British before winter. The Americans needed a navy to engage the enemy on the lake.

This huge and impossible task was handed to Benedict. He had vast sea experience and the tenacity to accomplish it, if it were at all possible. Benedict left quickly for the small port town of Skenesborough, where the new American shipyard was already in motion. Carpenters and ship builders converged there by the hundreds. Many skilled craftsmen from Pennsylvania, Massachusetts and Connecticut began the task of building the first American navy.

Supplies were short, but Benedict was good at managing details. He secured sailcloth, anchors, tar, brushes, cannons, ammunition and gunpowder. He also supervised construction details. To build and equip ships, work in the shipyard went on day and night. It was hoped that a respectable navy could be formed in just three to four weeks.

Benedict did have one distraction from his duties when Gates summoned him to Fort Ticonderoga for hearings on the earlier campaign season. Some of the junior officers Benedict had rubbed the wrong way wanted satisfaction. Benedict was prepared to settle these petty arguments by duel, if that was what they wanted.

Sometimes, Benedict's abrupt, no-nonsense manner got him into trouble and made bitter enemies within the ranks. He would have been smarter to pay more attention to political matters, as these small-minded officers did what they could to damage his reputation. Some of the officers cleared themselves of charges, and Benedict was also cleared, so Gates dissolved the court.

Benedict didn't let the distraction keep him from his duties, as he hurried back to Skenesborough to ready the fleet. Though the proceedings made him a bit resentful and angry, he threw himself back into his work—even harder—for the cause of liberty.

By late August of 1776, most of the fleet was ready for battle. The fleet consisted of nine gundalows—flat-bottomed, single-masted craft with fixed, square sails.

They could only move with the wind. Other movement depended on men rowing with oars. The boats were about 50 feet in length and held a crew of 45 men. Each gundalow was equipped with three to five cannons and up to eight swivel guns. They were christened The Boston, Connecticut, Jersey, New Haven, New York, Philadelphia, Providence, Spitfire and Success.

Also ready for service were three row galleys. These were more maneuverable craft. They were 70 to 80 feet in length, with two short masts that had swiveling triangular sails. The row galleys could tact with the wind, but also had oars for calm conditions.

The row galleys had quarterdecks and cabins. They were equipped with eight to ten cannons and up to 16 swivel guns. The craft were christened Congress, Trumbull and Washington. Another part of the fleet were the sloops Enterprise and Liberty. They had been seized during the prior campaign season, when Benedict first entered the region.

Two more ships, the cutters Lee and Royal Savage, were ships seized by General Montgomery at St. Johns during the start of the Canadian campaign. These schooners accommodated up to 50 men, three to four cannons and up to ten swivel guns. By late August, Benedict had a fleet of 17 warships ready for battle. He wanted twice that number, but he knew that time and the enemy would soon be pressing upon his troops.

To add to the fleet's problems were the lack of experienced sailors. Many men were available, but they didn't want to face the storms or the enemy on the water. The army drew lots to see who would serve in the navy.

Although Benedict had extensive maritime experience, most of his crews had little to none. He also lacked experienced artillery fighters. Before he could set sail, he had to find a ship's surgeon. To make matters worse, there was an extreme shortage of gunpowder. The fleet they were about to face had much larger artillery and ships, navigated by professional, experienced sailors.

As the patriot fleet was frantically preparing, the British were at the north end of the lake, doing the same. They dismantled warships on the St. Lawrence and moved them to St. Johns for re-assembly. They were also building more ships and bateaus at their shipyard.

Benedict pushed on, night and day, getting ships ready while drilling and training his men how to sail and use artillery. As preparations got closer to completion, General Gates set up a meeting with his commodore Benedict. He informed Benedict that the fleet was to be used as a defensive action only, which certainly wasn't in Benedict's nature. If he engaged the enemy, he was to inflict as much damage as possible to slow them down, then retreat to help defend Fort Ticonderoga, hopefully with minimal loss of life or arms.

Battle preparations were underway to face Carlton and Burgoyne. The American mission was to try and halt any progress south by the British until the next campaign season. The Americans' hope was to re-group and try to fight the British off the next spring or summer. Victory against the overwhelming force was not a reasonable expectation.

Benedict's fleet set sail in late August of 1776. Halfway up the lake, progress was going quite well when a fierce storm with gale force winds crashed into the fleet. Benedict gave orders for a southward retreat. The gundalow ship, "The Spitfire," didn't react in time to fend off the strong winds. Surging waves pushed the ship toward shore and certain destruction.

Realizing the ship was in serious trouble, Benedict jumped into a small boat and directed his very frightened oarsman to row him toward The Spitfire. Through a speaking horn, he screamed orders to the ship's captain, giving him instructions of how to trim the sails properly. The ship soon swung about and avoided any damage. His men commented on Benedict's fearless behavior. They knew they had a leader they could look up to and respect.

The fleet made it to a bay and relative safety from the storm. At least, they had passed their first test as seamen. A grateful Benedict called his men together and they went to shore to celebrate. They enjoyed a good meal and drank toasts to the health of Congress and Benedict. They proclaimed the spot they stood on as "Arnold's Point," in honor of their commodore.

As the weather cleared and the lake calmed down, they set sail north again, toward the enemy. Benedict surveyed the islands and coves along the way, looking for any structures in the lake that could give them some advantage in battle.

By September 3rd of 1776, they reached their northern destination and had yet to encounter any sign of their enemies. Benedict sent out scouting craft and put the fleet in battle formation across the lake. He wanted the British to know they wouldn't sail down Lake Champlain without a fight. They at least won the race to enter the lake, but knew the invading force would be preparing to engage.

The British and Indian allies formed a raiding party and attacked one of Benedict's ships that was closest to the shore. The brave crew drove them off, but lost three men and sustained six wounded. Sentries posted along the shore noticed enemy activity. Benedict recognized the British were planning to attack the fleet with land artillery and ships, simultaneously. He then ordered the fleet a few miles south to ruin their plan.

Benedict received intelligence of the enemy's strength. They had one ship alone capable of carrying 18 cannons. He needed some kind of advantage and found it in a bay by Valcour Island. He thought, as the British fleet sailed down the main channel, he could ambush them from the bay. By the time the Brits could make a turn into the wind and react to his fleet, he could do much damage to their rear guard, maybe even sinking row galleys that would be carrying thousands of their soldiers.

If Benedict's idea worked and they survived the battle, they could still swing south toward Ticonderoga. They anchored the small fleet in Valcour Bay in a half-moon battle formation and Benedict continued training his men. In a sense, they had already accomplished part of their mission, slowing the British down, as they now knew they couldn't sail the whole Champlain corridor without resistance.

Benedict, while nervously waiting for the enemy on-slaught, sent messages to General Gates. He requested more experienced seamen and more gunpowder. Gates replied, saying the supplies requested just weren't available, and also informed him that Washington was engaging the enemy near New York City. Benedict knew he would have his own hands full at any minute.

The minutes turned into weeks. The British were taking their time in preparations, as they wanted to be sure they had all capability to destroy any resistance. September passed and the leaves were beginning to show their bright fall colors. The temperature dropped and Benedict had to request more clothing for his men. Food stores were also getting low. It had to be torture, knowing that 850 cold, wet sailors were about to face nearly 7,000 well-supplied troops.

On October 10th of 1776, Benedict called for a council of war. He called his officers together to go back over the battle plans. One of the officers suggested, on seeing Carlton's fleet, that they retreat toward Fort Ticonderoga and engage the enemy along the way. Benedict knew that was what the British expected them to do. He also knew they would easily out sail the smaller patriot ships and blow them out of the water.

Benedict's plan was quite unconventional. He said he would let some of the British fleet pass by the island's bay. He would keep his ships in a tight, crescent-shaped formation and attack from the side and rear. The British would have to make long turns into the wind to engage the American fleet. With the hope of Providence, he thought his seamen could inflict enough damage to escape or drive the British back toward Canada for repairs. He told his men he would be giving orders and directions from the middle of the crescent and he assigned the officers he wanted on his left and right flanks.

As the council of war broke up, Benedict gave his most chilling instructions. He told his men to make sure to cover the powder magazines with wet blankets to keep hot lead and sparks from exploding them, and also to spread sand on the ships' decks so the men would keep their footing in any pools of blood.

Benedict's plan did have some serious flaws. He was counting on the overconfidence of the British navy and assumed they wouldn't send any scouting craft to search for enemy vessels. Also, if the wind was in their favor, they could turn quickly into the bay, trapping his fleet or drop anchor and foil any attempt of escape. He had to make sure the British would engage in battle on his terms.

On October 11th of 1776, Benedict's assumption of British overconfidence proved correct. He could see their lead ships in the channel, moving south without any scouting vessels. He waited patiently until part of the fleet sailed past the island and when the wind was right, he gave orders to drop sails and quickly sailed toward the enemy, offering volleys of cannon fire. The Battle of Valcour Island had begun.

Benedict's plans went perfectly. With the wind in his favor, the little American fleet inflicted major damage to the Royal Navy. Gun smoke filled the air and wood splinters covered the cold waters of Lake Champlain. The battle roared on, with both sides delivering damaging strikes from about 11 a.m. to dusk. Benedict kept himself highly visible to encourage his men, shouting orders and directing fire, even aiming many of the cannons on his ship himself. His face was blackened with burnt gunpowder.

By nightfall, the battle had ended pretty much in a draw. Both sides caused extensive loss to the other, but neither was overpowered. There were about 60 casualties on each side, with many wounded. The British couldn't believe they could not sweep this little navy aside, nor could they believe how much tenacity Benedict and his men had showed in battle.

While the battle raged, many Redcoats and Indian allies worked themselves over to Valcour Island, lining the shoreline and hoping to catch the Americans in a crossfire. Benedict managed to keep his fleet just out of their range. The only part of Benedict's plan that went awry was when the sun set and the battle ended. His fleet was hopelessly trapped in Valcour Bay.

The enemy controlled the shorelines and the British fleet was controlling the end of the bay in battle formation. The British and Benedict knew that by sun up, the American fleet would have to surrender or face annihilation. But that evening, Providence stepped in.

It was a dark, cold fall night and heavy fog rolled into the Champlain Valley. Benedict decided to try a breakout. He ordered the wounded be put into cabins to muffle their groans. A lantern was mounted on the stern of each ship, with the side toward the British fleet covered. Benedict ordered the oarsmen to row as silently as possible.

Single file, with each ship following the lantern of the other, they rowed silently between the British fleet and the New York shoreline. As the sun rose, the British were about to savor their victory. But when the fog lifted from the lake, the whole American fleet was gone! Carlton was furious!

The crippled—but still alive—American fleet sailed quickly toward Crown Point and Fort Ticonderoga all night. The very embarrassed British fleet set sail in pursuit. Benedict had a good head start, but the wind was favoring the British ships. In order to preserve what was left of his fleet, Benedict decided to turn back to the north and engage the enemy. He had one other warship and three gundalows with him. He knew a narrow spot in the lake called Split Rock, and decided to make a stand there.

The captain of Benedict's other warship was soon surrounded by three British vessels and took some nasty broadside shots. Many of his men were wounded, so he struck his colors and surrendered.

The British then concentrated on Benedict's ship. The royal fleet had five times the firepower Benedict had, as they paid no attention to the smaller gundalows.

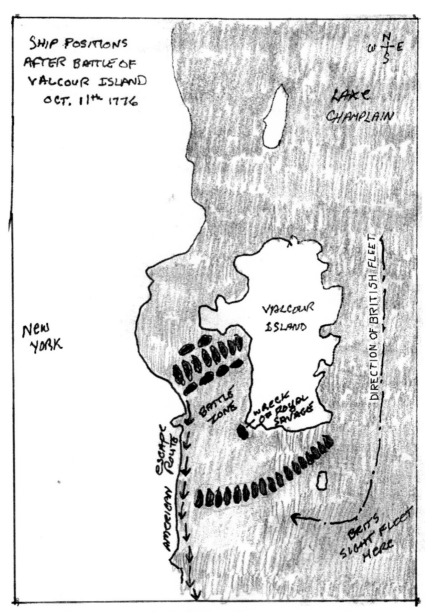

Ship positions after Battle of Valcour Island

Cannons trained on Benedict's men. The angry British would have their prize and revenge.

Benedict proved he was an expert at maneuvering ships, relying on his experiences of sailing from the West Indies to Canada. Somehow, he managed to engage the British fleet for a full two hours. He knew the British would be overconfident, and as the battle raged, he studied his position and the shoreline, waiting for the right moment.

The British commander could not believe that Benedict refused to strike his colors and surrender. His ship was pinned broadside, with two warships and another at his stern, firing relentless grapeshot and cannon balls. Benedict later wrote that his men fought back "briskly."

At the perfect moment of position, Benedict shouted to his men to quickly take their places on the oars. He passed between two of the very surprised British warships. They were at a point where they couldn't turn and catch the wind. Benedict called to the gundalows to do the same and follow him. They rowed quickly into a cove and grounded the ships.

Surprised, the British tried desperately to maneuver and catch them with cannon fire. Benedict had the men and wounded quickly unloaded and used what was left of the gunpowder to blow up the ships and keep them from the enemy. They made their way by land toward Fort Ticonderoga, skirting around Indian raiding parties.

Benedict finally arrived at Fort Ticonderoga at 4 a.m. on October 14th of 1776. It would be the first sleep his Champlain veterans had in three days.

At Fort Ticonderoga, which was now better reinforced, Benedict's navy prepared for a massive British onslaught, which never materialized. The fledgling American navy had completely accomplished its mission. By now, it was so late in the campaign season that the Brits decided to fall back to Canada and regroup. They would have to put off their assault at least until spring.

Benedict should have gone down in history as "Father of the American Navy."

CHAPTER FOURTEEN

An Uneasy Winter of '76

Benedict's reputation was spreading throughout the colonies and even back to England. The tenacity of this "horse jockey" from Connecticut was unbelievable.

Governor Carlton, out of respect for such bravery and also as a means to conserve rations and spread dissent among the American troops, sent British warships under a flag of truce to Fort Ticonderoga. He turned over his captured prisoners of war.

By mid-November of 1776, the Americans knew the Champlain region and Fort Ticonderoga would be safe, at least until spring. The generals released the militia who came to help defend the old fort. The generals then traveled to Albany to confer with General Schuyler, and on November 21st of 1776, they granted the regular army troops furloughs to go home, at least for a while.

October and November of 1776 weren't going well at all for George Washington. He retreated from Manhattan and his army suffered heavy casualties. They fought hard against General Howe's forces in the Battle of White Plains, but to no avail. Washington had to retreat farther west. The enemy had captured over 100 cannons in Manhattan, along with thousands of muskets and other weaponry. They also lost Fort Lee in New Jersey to General Cornwallis.

Washington suffered 3,000 casualties in the two defeats. In late November, he abandoned the New York area and moved his forces west toward the Delaware River.

In a desperate situation, Washington was in full retreat across New Jersey. He wrote to the northern army for reinforcements. Schuyler and Gates held back furloughs on eight regiments, since their enlistment times were still good until January 1st. Gates marched south to help relieve Washington.

Benedict wanted desperately to go home and see his boys, who he hadn't seen in 16 months. He wanted to see how his sister, Hannah, was managing with the boys and attend to the business affairs she was also helping with. He mentioned to Gates and Schuyler that he needed to settle some "public accounts" and that he wished to go home, at least for a while.

But Benedict's sense of duty and honor steered him in

another direction. Knowing of Washington's dire situation, he sailed down the Hudson River, secured a horse and rode hard to reach Washington's camp. He arrived at Washington's headquarters before Gates and the Ticonderoga divisions. While on his journey, he had received a letter from Washington that was almost a week old. George had given him orders to hurry toward New England, as he had heard Rhode Island was invaded by the British. By the time he got the letter, he was almost at Washington's camp, so he went there first.

On about December 21st of 1776, Benedict discussed the military situation with Washington, and being offensive minded, he suggested to his Excellency that he should make use of his troops before January 1st—when their enlistments would run out—just as he and Montgomery had been forced to do in Quebec.

The following day, Benedict made haste toward New England. The journey would at least allow him to return home to New Haven, if only for a brief visit. On about New Year's Day, Benedict arrived home to see his boys and sister, Hannah. He couldn't believe how much his sons had grown. They wanted to hear his tales of adventures.

Hannah gave him the bad news that his accounts were dwindling due to the war, besides his own purse, which he was draining constantly in the war effort. The British navy had curtailed shipping. Merchants like John

Hancock and Benedict were reduced to smuggling to avoid bankruptcy.

As news that Benedict was in New Haven traveled through town, many neighbors and citizens turned out to give him a warm welcome. His new-found hero status was heralded throughout New England. Benedict appreciated the warm welcome and rejoiced at some more great news. He had been petitioning Washington and Congress to put his Kennebec warriors, especially Daniel Morgan and his riflemen, on the earliest prisoner exchange lists. He finally got the good news that they had been released from the Quebec prison.

Morgan received a colonel's commission and went on to revive his band of Virginia riflemen. Another officer under Benedict's command, John Lamb, was also given a colonel's commission and was assigned by Congress the task of forming a second continental artillery regiment. But Congress wouldn't or couldn't appropriate the funds necessary. Out of his own funds, Benedict gave Lamb the money he needed. Lamb was a friend of Benedict's who suffered a bad facial wound during the Battle of Quebec.

Such affection and appreciation for troops was a rare commodity, but not with Benedict. He was a very different sort of general. He had to keep his visit at home short. By January 12th of 1777, he arrived in Providence, Rhode Island to assess the situation.

While in Rhode Island, Benedict received some more happy news. He found out Washington used his advice to begin offensive operations before enlistments ran out. Washington launched a Christmas Eve raid on British outposts in Trenton and was victorious. He also captured Princeton a few days later. Finally, George had accomplished something positive in the war effort.

Gates had advised Washington to retreat to the Pennsylvania mountains and take until spring to regroup. He didn't think it was wise to initiate these offensive operations. He especially didn't like Washington taking advice or influence from Benedict.

Horatio Gates faked an illness and left his men with Washington. He then traveled to Congress and began a nasty smear campaign, not only against Benedict, but also Washington. He hoped to use his upper class status to possibly even replace Washington with himself. If it weren't for George's victories at Trenton and Princeton, it may have worked. Had Washington not taken Benedict's advice, he probably would have been replaced as commander-in-chief.

While in Rhode Island, Benedict found the British were entrenched in Newport and had full control of the port there. But being in the middle of a New England winter, they were showing no signs of moving offensive operations toward Providence, nor toward any rebel positions.

Benedict wanted to spring an attack and try to drive the enemy out of Newport and back to New York City, or even Great Britain. But many enlistments had run out and he had not nearly the troop strength necessary to do anything other than hold his position in Providence. Since the British weren't doing anything offensively, Benedict decided he would ride to Boston to see if he could bolster enlistments to get volunteers and find financial support for a campaign.

In Boston, he was surprised to be received as quite a celebrity, as news of his exploits had preceded him. His new stature went a little bit to his head. He thought he should update his uniform, so he made a visit to Paul Revere's shop. He ordered new epaulets, along with a sword knot, a sash, a two-belt apparatus and one dozen silk hose. He thought if he was going to mingle with New England's elite, he should look the part.

Benedict attended social gatherings and gala balls, trying to build support for the "cause." He became quite infatuated with a Boston debutante named Elizabeth DeBlois. She was an attractive daughter of a wealthy Boston merchant. He hoped to court and possibly even marry her. He sent gifts and did what he could to gain her affection.

Now an infamous military leader, Benedict was dreaming of a new America, one where ability, achievement and virtuous service would be a measure of a citizen's worth. He hoped for an "aristocracy of talent," rather than one based on class and money. He would prove to be quite naïve and idealistic in his thinking. Benedict lingered in Boston until nearly March, in his efforts to win Miss DeBlois and raise support for the revolution.

Benedict then made his way back to Providence. He resolved that a defensive strategy was his only option, at least until late spring. While there, he received information that Congress and Washington were making preparations to gear up for the coming campaign season. He wondered where he would be asked to serve.

As he prepared his troops and defenses around Providence, Benedict received some devastating news. He normally ignored all the political wrangling of Congress, but he didn't know that others—like Gates—were stabbing him in the back politically. The elites in Congress gave out assignments and promotions to many, except Benedict.

Benedict expected and deserved to receive a command position, hoping it would be in the northern department. But Congress completely passed him over. Washington even wrote to him, saying Congress must have made a "mistake." Benedict thought his virtuous service and battle wounds would be enough, but Congress deeply wounded him worse than the bullet had.

He angrily decided he would ride to Congress, resign his commission and defend his honor. He left a General

Spencer in charge of the defensive operations in Providence and rode back home to New Haven.

On his arrival home, Benedict told his sister, Hannah, that he would soon be a civilian and he intended to be back soon to help her rebuild the business. His decision to resign from the army gave him some calm, as he could—at least—spend more time with his sons.

While in New Haven, Benedict diligently put together his public accounts of the past campaign season, as he funded a great deal of his efforts from his own pocket. He was looking forward to reviving his business and was quite bitter toward the elites in Congress. As he readied to go to Philadelphia to resign and regain his honor, he got some sad news. His courtship proposals to Miss DeBlois had been rejected.

CHAPTER FIFTEEN

The "Cause" of Liberty—Above All Else

Winter faded and the first signs of spring were beginning to show in April of 1777. A sad and bitter Benedict rode his horse toward Philadelphia. So much was going through his mind—how he was going to present his resignation, how to revive his merchant business and how much his family needed him at home.

Suddenly, a courier galloped toward him with shocking news. A large British detachment had landed in Norwalk, Connecticut—some 30 miles from Benedict's home—and was marching toward Danbury, the site of a major patriot supply depot. His sense of duty and value of "liberty's cause" overrode his personal problems. Benedict yet again prepared for combat.

Benedict rode hard toward Danbury. As he passed the homes of residents, he put out a call to muster any available militia to Danbury immediately. He arrived late in the evening of a cold, rainy April night.

General Sullivan, the local militia commander, was found at nearby Redding. Sullivan provided the details of the day's events for General Arnold. Also showing up was old General David Wooster, who Benedict had to contend with in Quebec. Sullivan explained what he knew. That day, a British commander, "Tryon," had landed in Norwalk by ships, with a huge British raiding party. Mostly British infantry and a battalion of Loyalists, numbering 2,000 strong, were marching straight inland toward Danbury.

The continental troops stationed to protect the supply depot numbered only about 150 men. They found out about the advancing force, hid what supplies they could, and were forced to retreat into the countryside.

Tryon ordered his troops to destroy everything in their path. They destroyed all the supplies they found, then proceeded to burn some 40 homes and buildings. By day's end, all of Danbury was burning. The British hoped also to crush the rebels' will to fight, but their actions only filled the rebels with resolve and hatred.

The rebel generals agreed on that very cold and rainy night to move in closer to the raiding party with their militias, who were now numbering nearly 600 men— with hopefully more on the way. They could see the glowing embers of what was left of Danbury at about 2 a.m. Benedict told the men to dry their gunpowder and be prepared to see action at dawn.

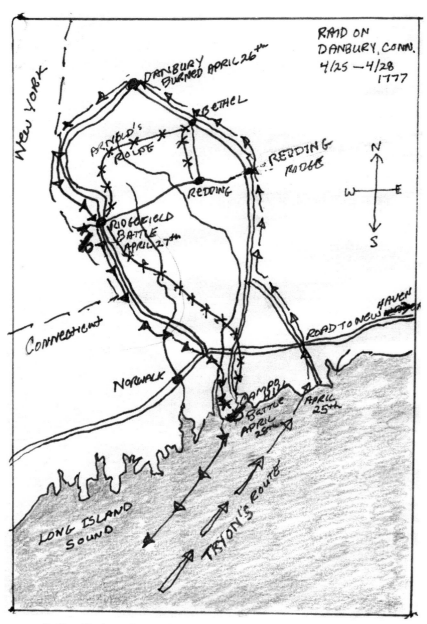

Raid on Danbury, Connecticut

Benedict thought he was outnumbered nearly three to one. He planned on cutting the raiding party off before they could reach the sea. He assumed they would be heading back to their ships in Norwalk or possibly to Tarrytown on the coast, to destroy it also. The small village of Ridgefield would be a possible interception point. An emergency war council was held.

It was agreed there would be a plan to have General Wooster and his son attack the rear guard of the British column with about 200 of the men. Benedict would take the remaining 400 and make a line at Ridgefield, directly challenging the enemy. As Benedict quickly marched toward Ridgefield, he picked up another 100 militia.

At 11 a.m. on that very morning, Wooster attacked the rear guard of the British column with about 200 of the men. Benedict would take the remaining 400 and make a line at Ridgefield, directly facing the enemy. The British turned and charged at Wooster's American force. Wooster was suddenly hit in the groin by a musket ball as he ordered a retreat. His son tried to help him up, but he was impaled by a bayonet. Wooster died painfully five days later, giving up his and his son's lives for the cause of liberty.

Wooster's actions gave Benedict's men valuable time to ready their positions. The British column came into view at about 3 p.m. Benedict's men waited nervously in Ridgefield, taking cover behind wagons and stone walls. The British made a frontal attack, but the rebel lines held steady with Benedict's encouragement. Frustrated that they couldn't break the rebel position, the Brits sent out flanking parties, seeing they had superior numbers. The flanking maneuvers were working, causing the rebel lines to break up and flee.

Benedict brandished his sword and rode desperately back and forth, trying to form a rear guard to protect the fleeing troops. His horse suddenly dropped to the ground, thrashing in pain. Benedict's mount was hit with nine musket balls and the commander was pinned beneath. As Benedict was trying to free himself from the throws of the dying animal, a British soldier rushed toward him, ordering him to surrender, screaming, "You are my prisoner!" Benedict was heard to reply, "Not yet." He pulled his pistol and killed the soldier with one shot. He struggled free from under the horse and limped away toward a nearby swamp. Shots were raining all around him and he barely got away.

Tryon never thought he would meet so much resistance. He decided to stop the attack and regroup. That night, he made camp in Ridgefield, to tend to the dead and wounded. There were still 15 miles to get back to the coast.

Benedict found another horse, and never sleeping, he worked all night assembling his men and going through the countryside to try and rally more help. He was still hopelessly outnumbered. He knew there were only two roads Tryon could take to get back to his ships. Unfortunately, some Loyalists warned Tryon where they saw the American force assembling. Early the next morning, Tryon moved his men farther north to skirt around Benedict's force.

With such low numbers of soldiers, Benedict decided to try and hit the side and rear of the British column, using hit and run tactics. Benedict constantly exposed himself to enemy fire to encourage his men. The British made it to a point called Campo Hill near the coast, which gave them an advantage against the attack. They also gained reinforcements from the ships, including some artillery.

When Benedict formed lines of aggression, one witness later wrote about the event, saying, "Arnold continually exposed himself, almost to a fault," and reportedly, "exhibited the greatest marks of bravery, coolness and fortitude under fire." Benedict rode up the front of the lines, ignoring the heavy musket fire and grapeshot. He was heard to shout, "By the love of themselves, posterity and all things sacred, do not desert me!"

The rebel line finally broke, as the British charged down the hill. A musket ball ripped through the collar of Benedict's coat. Then, his horse took a hit to the neck and it went down. Somehow, Benedict survived with only bruises. Tryon's force easily escaped to the waiting ships.

The Americans had made quite an impressive stand, for their numbers. Benedict's old Kennebec friend, John Lamb, whose artillery unit he had funded, managed to get some artillery pieces into the battle, but Lamb himself was wounded with grapeshot. It was the second time Lamb was hurt while fighting under Benedict. He had already lost an eye in Quebec. Benedict wrote of the engagement, never speaking of his own actions. He related how "Many of the officers and men had behaved well."

The news of Tryon's raid and Benedict's heroism quickly reached Congress. Many of the congressmen felt quite embarrassed that this American hero had just been passed over for promotion. On May 2nd of 1777, they quickly promoted Benedict to Major General. John Hancock sent word of the promotion on to Washington with a message that Benedict's behavior was "highly approved by Congress."

John Adams went much further. In those desperate times, America needed a hero. The army's enlistment quotas were falling far short of what was needed.

Adams requested that a medal be struck in Benedict's honor. He went into great detail. On one side, he wanted: "A platoon firing at General Arnold on horseback, his horse falling dead under him and he deliberately disentangled his feet from the stirrups and taking his pistols out of his holsters before the retreat." On the other side of the medal, he wrote that he wanted: "Arnold should be mounted on a fresh horse, receiving another discharge of musketry with a wound in the horse's neck."

Congress felt Benedict would be satisfied with a Major Generalship, but they fell short of giving him seniority over the others they had promoted. So Benedict would have to serve under other soldiers he had commanded just months ago. Even Washington commented there must be something "amiss" in their thinking.

Benedict still felt quite frustrated and betrayed by politics and politically minded officers. He knew that while he had been giving his all in the field, others in Congress were busy slandering his name and his honor. He was determined to have full satisfaction, to the point of drawing pistols if necessary. He also had public accounts owed to him and he hoped for at least partial restitution.

As Benedict again set out for Philadelphia, he fully intended to resign his commission. He wasted no time in his quest to be heard by Congress. A very surprised George Washington received Benedict at his headquarters in Morristown, New Jersey on May 12th of 1777. Benedict requested permission to travel to Philadelphia, since no major actions were going on at the moment.

Washington wanted to keep his fighting general in the field and did his best to calm Benedict's manner down. He was in need of someone to command a supply depot in Peekskill, but Benedict would hear none of it.

At that point, Washington knew he—nor his army—could stop Benedict from going to Philadelphia. Washington penned a letter to John Hancock for Benedict to take to Congress. The letter addressed the seniority issue of Benedict's promotion and he wrote: "It is universally known" how Benedict had "always distinguished himself as a judicious, brave officer of good activity, enterprise and perseverance." He again counseled Benedict to remain composed.

CHAPTER SIXTEEN

The Political Arena—1777

Benedict arrived in Philadelphia on May 16th of 1777 and found lodging with the Maryland delegation and Representative Carroll, who had gone north to work with him in Montreal. He spent the weekend mingling with delegates to Congress. On Monday, May 19th, he entered the Pennsylvania State House, which some were now calling "Independence Hall."

He presented Washington's letter and his own complaints. The next day, Benedict insisted on a court of inquiry to clear any charges against his name, and requested his public accounts be settled.

The delegates actually caught Benedict off guard when they acted the very same day, offering him hearty thanks for his acts of heroism. His case was turned over to the Board of War for satisfaction. He was surprisingly honored with the gift of a horse, to replace the two shot from beneath him in Connecticut. They wrote, from a grateful nation, for his "gallant conduct." One of the delegates wrote of Benedict's appearance: "His face handsome" and his muscular stature as a man low in height, "but well made."

On May 22nd, the Board of War met with Benedict and poured over documentation relating to his public accounts. The next day, the board expressed "entire satisfaction," concerning the General's character and conduct, ordering their findings be published.

Though his spirits were buoyed by the actions of Congress, Benedict still had much anguish over the matter of seniority of rank. He continued to cajole the thinking of the delegates. Unfortunately, Congress—being mostly upper class—decided it best to dole out the rank of general based on class and influence, rather than merit or accomplishment.

Benedict wasn't the only general with issues for Congress. General Schuyler had many grievances to address, as did General Gates.

The political wrangling over the next month was nearly unbearable. John Adams wrote to his wife Abigail: "I am wearied to death with the wrangles between military officers, high and low. They quarrel like cats and dogs. They worry one another like Mastiffs, scrambling for rank and pay like apes for nuts." But he wouldn't admit that Congress was the cause of most of the wrangling.

Benedict was getting a belly full of colonial politics. He felt the aristocracy was out of touch with the general population and the military. He also thought they were far too indecisive and slow to act. He especially didn't care for the courting of the French. He let it be known that he didn't want to fight off one monarchy to get in bed with another.

With all of this going on, tension was building. It was well known that two extraordinarily large British armies were making plans to pounce on America from New York City and Canada. Everyone was speculating about when they would force their campaigns.

Washington kept busy developing a wide spy ring to see if he could glean information about British General Howe's intentions for attack. Washington also moved his men 20 miles south to Middlebrook Heights, a well-defensible mountainous region. Howe tried a luring tactic to get Washington's army onto flatter ground for a decisive battle.

Benedict rode determinedly toward Princeton, under orders to engage the enemy if necessary. It was to Benedict's liking, as he was always offensively minded. But Washington didn't take the bait and stayed entrenched in the mountains.

Howe, realizing the American army couldn't be taunted into the open, retreated back to New York City. The threat over, Benedict returned to Philadelphia. He entered Independence Hall on July 11th of 1777 and handed over his letter of resignation. He felt dishonored that he wasn't granted seniority and intended to go home to his family and business. Benedict said he would return at a later date to settle his public accounts.

Unknown to Benedict, Congress had just received an urgent communication from Washington. He wanted Benedict Arnold sent to him as soon as possible. Washington had received news that "Gentleman Johnny" Burgoyne had moved down Lake Champlain and captured Fort Ticonderoga. The looming force to the north was on the move.

The congressional delegates couldn't believe Washington didn't request General Gates. They didn't want to second-guess his thinking, since they needed immediate action.

Congress decided to disregard Benedict's resignation. John Hancock gave Benedict orders to immediately repair to Washington's headquarters and take all of Washington's directions.

Benedict said he would gladly go and fight as a private citizen. But Congress wouldn't hear of it. They were in urgent need of a fighting general and the seniority issue would have to wait. Benedict was in Washington's camp by July 17th of 1777. Reports were received that

Burgoyne's army was on the move and Benedict prepared to go to the northern theater. Over the following month, Benedict seemed to be almost everywhere.

CHAPTER SEVENTEEN

The Northern Threat to Crush American Resistance

General Burgoyne moved down from Canada with an intimidating force of nearly 10,000 troops. The huge army consisted of British regulars, Hessian mercenaries and Indian war parties. The Canadians weren't so supportive of the British, registering only 150 men.

Burgoyne traveled in the style becoming to a British major general of aristocracy. He drank champagne and traveled with his mistress and other lady cohorts. He was quite confident he would sweep away any resistance in the Champlain corridor. His plan was to march to Albany and wait in comfort for Howe to send more reinforcements from New York City. Burgoyne sent a second force under Colonel Barry St. Ledger through the western regions from Lake Ontario.

St. Ledger was to travel through the Mohawk Valley and link with Howe in Albany. He anticipated, after crushing any American resistance and meeting with General

"Gentleman" John Burgoyne, here shown in a portrait by the renowned Sir Joshua Reynolds, led the northern attack on America. He was later defeated at Saratoga, turning the tide of the war. General Benedict Arnold is credited with his defeat. *Courtesy, Library of Congress.*

Howe's army, America would be split, overpowered and the upstart rebellion would be over.

As Burgoyne made his move down Lake Champlain, Benedict's previous warning about reinforcing Mount Defiance came to pass. The commander left in charge of Fort Ticonderoga thought no army could possibly haul artillery up the steep, wooded slopes of Mount Defiance. But that's exactly what they did. The British artillery commander had a saying: Where a goat can go, a man can go, where a man can go, a cannon can go.

When the rebels saw the cannons easily trained down on their positions and the massive flotilla in the lake, they had no choice but to abandon the indefensible fort and flee into the countryside. The Americans did everything they could to slow Burgoyne's progress south. They dropped trees on the roadway and destroyed any usable bridges.

Burgoyne's tactics were totally ruthless. He sent Indian war parties ahead of his regular army. They burned homes and people. They also scalped and tortured local residents. Burgoyne thought the terrorism would weaken the resolve of the colonists, but it did the opposite. All local and state militias were spurred to take up arms.

General Schuyler asked Benedict to do whatever he could to slow the British army's progress. As they were totally overwhelmed and outnumbered, the only option for the patriots was to hit and run, then hope for more recruits and the reinforcements that would help them make some kind of stand.

The rough terrain of what is now called the Adirondacks did the most to slow the British down. Between Lake Champlain and Lake George, they had to haul their supplies, artillery and men through a challenging three-mile portage, as Lake George is nearly 200 feet higher in elevation than Lake Champlain. By the time they reached the end of Lake George, it had taken them close to three weeks.

Benedict and his men seemed to be in skirmishes almost everywhere in the lower Champlain region, on nearly a daily basis. On July 27th of 1777, one of Benedict's reports may have helped turn the tide of the war. He had encountered a horrible scene. He wrote a report about a beautiful, blond American girl named Jenny McCrea. He found her "scalped, stripped and butchered" by Burgoyne's Indian raiding parties. His description of that find became a rallying cry throughout the colonies and was one of the most talked about atrocities of the war.

The story spread like wildfire—surely embellished along the way—but it caused militia and regular enlistments in the army to increase substantially. As the rebel forces grew, Benedict became more hopeful at the prospect that they could actually find a way to stop or even defeat Burgoyne. Benedict was hoping his friend, Daniel Morgan, would arrive with his riflemen. He thought that with Morgan's help, they would make a remarkable stand.

Luckily, Burgoyne's progress was painfully slow, with such a large army to keep supplied, in addition to such wild and treacherous terrain. His pace was minimal. But Burgoyne wrote that he was having a "jolly time." Besides the staggering numbers of men, he also had 50 teams of oxen to haul artillery and supplies, along with some 500 horses. He had contracted to bring another thousand horses from Canada, but they still had not arrived. Heavy rain also impeded his movement. His supply lines were being stretched farther and farther without any contact from his southern reinforcements.

Burgoyne made a decision to launch a large raid into the nearby Vermont countryside, in an attempt to plunder much-needed supplies, horses and oxen. He sent a Colonel Baum with 750 soldiers he considered "lesser" troops, compared to his British regulars. They consisted of mostly Hessian mercenaries, Canadians, a few Loyalists and Indians. He thought this raid would accomplish two purposes. They would easily gain much-needed supplies and he was hoping to trick the American forces into thinking he was turning his army southeast toward New England.

The diversionary force, led by Baum, met a band of 1,500 New Hampshire militiamen. Some of them were Green Mountain Boys and they were led by militia General John Stark.

John Stark, like Benedict, was passed over for promotion by Congress. Feeling dishonored, he resigned his commission. He said he would serve the people, not Congress. But he did get a commission to head the New Hampshire militia and he gathered troops to hinder the progress of Burgoyne's army.

On August 16th of 1777, near Bennington, General Starks' militia crushed Burgoyne's diversion. Starks' forces only sustained 60 killed and wounded. The British force lost some 207 soldiers, including Colonel Baum himself. Countless more were wounded and over 700 were taken as prisoners. In this one daring action, Burgoyne's army was reduced by nearly 15 percent.

Burgoyne confidently pushed slowly forward toward Albany. He was hoping to be reinforced by St. Ledger or Howe when he arrived there. He still felt he had more than enough of an army to sweep away any rebel resistance.

General Schuyler's plan of putting Benedict in charge of hit and run, coupled with the supply line disruption by the New Hampshire militia under Stark, was seriously slowing the progress of the British army. Schuyler held a council of war on August 12th of 1777. Information concerning Barry St. Ledger's force, advancing from the west, became known.

St. Ledger had moved through Lake Ontario and planned on marching through the Mohawk Valley toward a rendezvous with Burgoyne in Albany. The only substantial fort in his way was Fort Stanwix, which he could have bypassed, but he decided to lay siege to the fort and its inhabitants.

The militia force in the area, known as the Tryon County Militia, was under the command of General Nicholas Herkimer. He gathered a column of men to try and break the siege of Fort Stanwix. Herkimer sent out orders to muster all patriots in the area and have them gather at Fort Dayton. Most of the militiamen were Palatine German farmers who had settled in the area.

Herkimer managed to gather about 800 men and was supported by a number of Oneida and Tuscarora Indians. On August 6th of 1777, near Oriskany, the militia was working their way up a steep ravine on the route to Fort Stanwix, when they were ambushed in the ravine by some of St. Ledger's army and a fierce band of Mohawk and Seneca Indians.

Joseph Brant, a famous Indian chief and orator, led the Indians. Brant was educated by Sir William Johnson, and had even spent time in England. He tried to convince the entire Iroquois Nation to fight as one with the British. He managed to get only the Senecas and Mohawks to take his side. Brant and the Mohawks led many raids in their effort to burn out the German settlers in the Mohawk Valley.

During the battle, Herkimer was wounded badly in the leg, but he still managed to direct the battle from beneath a tree, while smoking his pipe. The fighting was some of the most terrible in the war and it went on for nearly two hours. About 150 of the militia fell, many sustained wounds and some 50 were taken as prisoners. Many of the prisoners were tortured to death by the Senecas and Mohawks.

The Herkimer militia had to withdraw back to Fort Dayton. General Herkimer's leg was amputated and he died shortly afterward.

General Schuyler received the news of the bloody August 6th Battle of Oriskany. He related the sad information during his August 12th war council. If Fort Stanwix fell to St. Ledger, nothing could stop his march through the Mohawk Valley to Albany. The officers present at the emergency war council pressed Schuyler not to reduce their numbers, with Burgoyne's army looming just to the east.

Visibly angry, General Schuyler said he would lead

a detachment, himself, to relieve the settlers at Fort Stanwix. The ever-offensive Benedict piped up and volunteered to take on St. Ledger.

Schuyler felt relieved when Benedict spoke up and volunteered for the mission. He knew if anyone could accomplish the task, Benedict would find a way. Schuyler also knew that if Burgoyne made a thrust toward Albany, he would need Benedict's talents in the field to stop him. Schuyler decided to pull his army back 12 miles toward the Mohawk Valley, to a more defensible position. He sent Benedict to relieve Stanwix and, hopefully, stop St. Ledger.

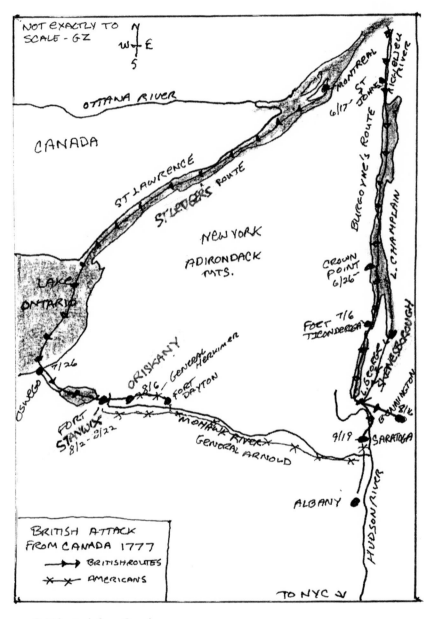

British attack from Canada

CHAPTER EIGHTEEN

The Dark Eagle

Benedict was given a brigade of 900 men and quickly proceeded west. He hoped to augment his forces with what remained of Herkimer's militia and the Indian allies of the Oneida and Tuscarora tribes. Keeping his army moving swiftly was essential, as they would be badly needed if Burgoyne launched an offensive.

Pushing his way rapidly toward Fort Dayton, Benedict planned on assembling there, in preparation for his offensive strike.

On August 21st of 1777, Benedict's officers requested a council of war. They had just received reliable intelligence about the size of St. Ledger's army. And, as usual, they were to be outnumbered two to one. The men wanted to wait for additional troops to arrive, especially after getting the details of the bloody battle at Oriskany.

Benedict knew there wasn't time to reinforce his men. Something had to be done before Burgoyne made another move. This was when one of the strangest events of the Revolution unfolded.

Benedict's reputation served him well on this occasion. He was known throughout the colonies, and especially in this region, as a formidable warrior general.

Indian tribes in the region, mainly the Iroquois—and others—had named Benedict "The Dark Eagle." His odd fighting style was one the Indians had never witnessed before. This general fought in front of his troops, swooping down on the enemy on horseback, with his sword drawn. They were reminded of an eagle zeroing in on its prey.

The Indians were accustomed to seeing generals directing battles from behind the lines and Benedict's aggressive fighting style struck fear in their hearts.

That very night, as the war council broke up, the mother and brother of a local Loyalist, Hon Yost Schuyler, approached Benedict. They pleaded with Benedict and begged him to spare Hon Yost's life. Hon Yost was under an order of execution by Tryon County officials.

Hon Yost had been caught recruiting Tory soldiers for St. Ledger's army. Benedict told Hon Yost's mother and brother that there was nothing he could do. In anguish, the mother pleaded with Benedict to at least speak with her son, who was in the prison at Fort Dayton.

Benedict went to the man's jail cell. He found Hon Yost to be a very strange and animated fellow. Some reports described him as half-witted. Today, there would probably be a psychological diagnosis for his condition, possibly acute bipolar disorder. But the Native American tribes respected his unusual behavior. They considered him "touched" by the "Great Spirit," and possibly even a prophet.

Hon Yost offered Benedict a plan, in exchange for his life. He said he would charge into St. Ledger's Indian camp and spread fear of General Arnold's mission to destroy them and St. Ledger's army, possibly even driving them off.

Strangely, Benedict approved of Hon Yost's plan, but to make sure he followed through with the ruse, he incarcerated Hon Yost's brother in his place. He also sent with Hon Yost a trusted Oneida scout to help with the deception and keep an eye on Hon Yost, in case he betrayed the plan.

A very thankful Hon Yost seemed to relish his role excitedly. He even shot holes in his clothing, so he looked like he had just escaped Benedict's clutches.

On August 22nd of 1777, Hon Yost ran breathlessly into the Indian camp near Fort Stanwix and wildly related his tale. He said the Dark Eagle would soon be there to crush them all. They asked how many men he had. Yost replied, "As many men as there are leaves on the trees!" The tribes panicked. They refused to face down the Dark Eagle, if he had that many men.

St. Ledger tried his best to calm the situation and called on the chiefs of the tribes to have a war council. But within a few hours, with Yost's help, the story had grown throughout the natives' camp. Some were saying Benedict had cut Burgoyne's army to pieces and was marching toward them with over 3,000 men.

When he wrote about the episode later, St. Ledger said the chiefs "grew furious" and "seized upon the officers' liquor and clothes." The Indians decamped, fleeing west into the Niagara frontier and leaving St. Ledger to fend for himself. Now, with half his force deserted, he made the decision to end the siege and fall back to Canada.

Benedict marched into Fort Stanwix, arriving on August 24th of 1777. The siege concluded without a shot. Benedict gave the fort's commander "great applause for their spirited conduct and vigorous defense."

Within four days, Benedict was back at Fort Dayton, preparing to move his now 1,200-man army down the Mohawk River to battle with Burgoyne.

CHAPTER NINETEEN

General Arnold at Saratoga:

"If the day is long enough, we'll have them all
in Hell before night!"

During the campaign season of 1777, Congress was in
a tither. The capital was moved to Baltimore because of
fears that Howe was going to make a move on Philadelphia. When Fort Ticonderoga fell in July, the leaders in
Congress were incensed. Washington was almost always
on the defensive and a scapegoat was needed to blame
for the loss of Fort Ticonderoga.

Congress was as much to blame as anyone, as they
never sent much-requested resources to supply the
northern army. The ax fell on General Schuyler. He
was made to take the blame for the devastating loss,
to the point of accusations of treason. Nothing could
have been further from the truth. Schuyler had accomplished even more than he possibly could, given
the resources available to him.

Between the activity of Benedict and Schuyler's work
with the Native Americans, there was still a fighting
chance in the north.

Congress called forth their darling, General Horatio Gates, to take command of the northern army. Gates was a well-established aristocrat like themselves, even though he had done little in the war effort except for fighting to advance himself. Congress was delighted with what they perceived to be a great decision.

Washington, even though he was an aristocrat himself, didn't trust Gates' constant quest for power. Schuyler handed over command to Gates on August 19th of 1777. Benedict made it back from Fort Stanwix to headquarters on August 30th of 1777. Gates needed Benedict to help formulate future action against Burgoyne's army.

With the weakening of British forces in Bennington and St. Ledger's retreat to Canada, the Americans knew Burgoyne would have to make a move toward Albany. Gates wrote to Congress to tell of the relief of Fort Stanwix and the driving off of St. Ledger's army. But not surprisingly, he never mentioned Benedict's role. The glory and success of the mission belonged to him and a few minor officers.

Benedict wasn't too happy his friend General Schuyler was replaced, especially with the likes of Gates. He also learned that Congress took up his seniority issue again and he was denied. But Benedict held his tongue. He had bigger fish to fry. He intended to prove his worth on the battlefield, in a decisive meeting with Burgoyne. He was starting to realize not all of his enemies were Redcoats.

"Gentleman Johnny" Burgoyne was in a bit of a pickle. His supply lines were too long and essentially cut off by the New Hampshire militia. Fifteen percent of his army was lost in his diversion, and now, the Indian allies he was relying on had reached the end of their agreed enlistments. Those Native Americans began to filter back to their homes.

Burgoyne still had a huge army of well-trained British regulars and a large group of Hessian mercenaries. He was considering either a full-scale retreat to Canada, or whether to cross the Hudson River and make a push toward Albany. He thought if he made it to Albany he could—realistically—get reinforced by Howe's army in New York City.

The very thought of retreat, with a rebel army nipping at his heels, was totally unappealing. He also had no respect for the rebel army and thought they would only fight defensively against such large numbers of battle-hardened and well-trained troops. His opinion of the rebel army was that they were a bunch of undisciplined bumpkins and no match for him.

Burgoyne made his push across the Hudson River on September 12th of 1777. It took two days to get his artillery and supplies across. He actually landed on property owned by General Schuyler. The British army plundered the ripe grain and food they found there, to feed the men and their horses. One officer wrote that the general's holdings "were reduced to a scene of distress and poverty."

Meanwhile, the American army was busy preparing to do battle. Tension grew between Benedict and Gates. Benedict pushed to have one large offensive strike and a decisive battle with Burgoyne. Gates, holding the command position, thought the only chance to defeat Burgoyne would be to entrench his lines from a better position and let Burgoyne dictate his own movements. It was exactly what Burgoyne hoped the rebels would do.

Benedict, not holding the higher rank, had to quell his feelings. Gates sent him on a mission to look for the best defensive grounds. He was sent with a Polish engineer, Thaddeus Kosciuszko. His expertise was used to determine strategic elevation and range for artillery. Thaddeus and Benedict agreed on the best site, four miles north of the their present position, at a place known as Bemis Heights.

The Heights were an expanse of high, rolling hills rising out of the plain near the Hudson River. From the Heights, they could reach the British with artillery. They were also protected by heavy woods and ravines to the west. For any type of frontal assault, the enemy would have to forge uphill.

On the very same day that Burgoyne made his move across the Hudson, the American army was setting up its new position at Bemis Heights.

Benedict was given command of the left wing, with many divisions of close to 3,000 men. The right wing was given to General John Glover. Gates set up headquarters in a small farmhouse at the center of the staging area. Trenches were dug and breastworks for artillery were constructed.

As Benedict prepared his wing for battle, his friend Daniel Morgan arrived the same day Benedict returned from Fort Stanwix. He brought with him 331 of his riflemen. Benedict was also glad to have many of his Kennebec warriors with him again. He was grateful to have so many battle-savvy men at his side. They knew what they were about to face.

Benedict, not knowing most of the Indians fighting for the British had gone back to their homes, assigned Morgan to be farthest to the west in the woods and open areas. The Americans knew Morgan and Benedict would be first to engage any enemy attack from their respective positions.

The American army was growing in strength daily. More and more men from New York, New England and elsewhere were filtering into the different divisions. From scouting reports, Burgoyne knew that. He realized he had to make a push toward Albany as soon as possible. On September 15th of 1777, the British army advanced south toward Albany, but was slowed because of bridges destroyed weeks before by General Schuyler.

By September 17th, the British reached a place called Sword's Farm, about four miles north of Bemis Heights. General Gates called for another war council that day. Benedict begged for orders to let his wing go out and assess the enemy's strength. Gates relented, since he needed the intelligence, but ordered Benedict not to press full engagement.

At the dawn of a foggy, fall morning, Benedict led his men—close to 3,000—in a northeasterly sweep toward the encamped British force. There were some small, bloody encounters, but Benedict did not press a battle.

Burgoyne wrote: "The enemy appeared in considerable force." He believed it was to obstruct bridge repair and draw him into a wooded area where he couldn't use his artillery. Late that afternoon, Benedict pulled his troops back to Bemis Heights and reported the day's events to Gates. Benedict's assessment was that the enemy would assault Bemis Heights within 48 hours, most likely by trying to flank his position in the left wing.

Gates shrugged off Benedict's assessment. He was sure Burgoyne would concentrate his movements along the road by the river. Burgoyne formulated his attack plan.

He decided he would split his army into three battle groups.

One group, under General Simon Fraser, would split out toward the ridge line angling southward, taking with him fast moving troops, sharpshooters and light artillery. Burgoyne would send a lighter group along the river road with his supplies, so the Americans would think he was going to push them along the river. The third and largest group, consisting mainly of British regulars, would turn into the American position on Bemis Heights.

Burgoyne assumed American troops would not risk any kind of offensive attack and would hold to their entrenched defensive positions. If they remained entrenched, he would soon have them in a deadly cross-fire and rout them out. He also assumed that if they did try an offensive strike, they would come up against his main thrust of British regulars.

What Burgoyne didn't know was that his plan was leading him into the most battle-hardened American troops fighting under Benedict. Also, his field general, Fraser, would come into direct contact with Daniel Morgan's riflemen. Burgoyne's main advance was aimed directly into Benedict's left wing.

On the morning of September 19th, a very cool, heavy fog settled into the Hudson River Valley. It was perfect cover for Burgoyne to launch his full charge into action. A rumble of cannon fire would be the signal for the three columns to begin their advance.

Benedict begged Gates for permission to send out Morgan's riflemen to probe the enemy and assess their attack plan. He kept pushing Gates, warning him that if the enemy weren't faced, Burgoyne could get artillery close enough to reach Bemis Heights. Gates, who the men had nicknamed "Granny Gates," was plagued with indecision. He finally relented to Benedict's pleading.

After getting Gates to make a decision, Benedict rushed to his horse and rode into action. He rode first to Daniel Morgan's position and sent his riflemen northwest to find the enemy's position. British General Fraser—with his division—was pushing hard to get around the top of a deep ravine. He was trying to get his men and artillery ready to advance along the ridgeline to Bemis Heights.

Burgoyne's regulars had to skirt around the bottom of the same ravine. They had agreed that when each division was ready for the full assault, they would signal each other with cannon fire. Their respective maneuvers took them until nearly noon, and the morning fog was no longer hiding their actions.

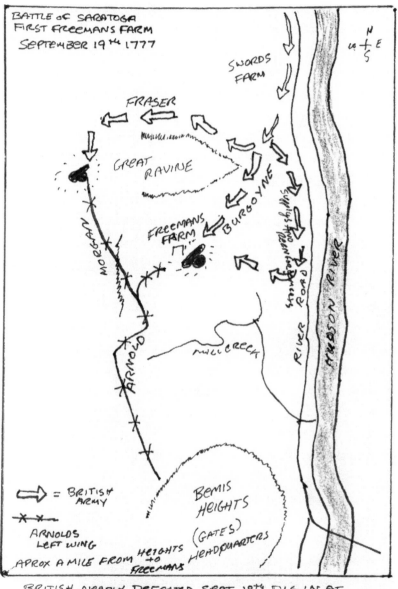

BATTLE of SARATOGA
FIRST FREEMANS FARM
SEPTEMBER 19th 1777

SWORDS FARM

N
W + E
S

FRASER

GREAT RAVINE

MORGAN

FREEMANS FARM

BURGOYNE

Sending two Reinforcements

RIVER ROAD

HUDSON RIVER

ARNOLD

MILL CREEK

⟹ = BRITISH ARMY

×—×—× ARNOLDS LEFT WING

BEMIS HEIGHTS
(GATES)
HEADQUARTERS

APROX A MILE FROM HEIGHTS to FREEMANS

BRITISH NEARLY DEFEATED SEPT. 19th DIG IN AT
FREEMANS FARM / FINAL BATTLE OCTOBER 7th 1777

The main thrust of the British army was converging on some open ground known as Freeman's Farm. The farm was about 20 cleared acres that still had numerous stumps and a log home surrounded by heavy woods. The farm was about a mile from Bemis Heights.

Burgoyne never dreamed the American army would dare to launch an offensive battle. But Benedict had already decided he had no intentions of letting Burgoyne dictate his movements. He would use his wing to disrupt Burgoyne's battle plans. Just past noon, Benedict could hear Morgan's riflemen firing on Fraser's column. He quickly sent two divisions to reinforce Morgan's men.

Benedict noticed a gap at Freeman's Farm, between the two British columns. He now knew he had his battle-field. Around 2 o'clock, Benedict led his first charge into Fraser's flank. He was repelled, but gave them considerable damage. He then wheeled to the right against the other British column. For the next three hours, the American army forced up to six charges into the British positions and also fended off counter charges.

It was one of the hardest fought battles of the American Revolution. Reports of Benedict's part in the battle showed he was almost everywhere, leading the front of the charges. Some soldiers wrote of the battle: "He acted like a madman." Some wrote that his voice rang "clear as a trumpet." He called on his men to follow him and "hurled them like a tornado into the British lines."

Another man wrote of Benedict's actions: "Nothing could exceed the bravery of Benedict on this day... There seemed to shoot out of him a magnetic force that electrified his men and made heroes of all within his influence."

As smoke from the cannon fire and muskets filled the valley that day, Benedict had employed his whole wing of 3,000 men in the two British columns by late afternoon. By sunset, Benedict could smell victory and he was sure one more aggressive charge would finish off the British columns. He rode furiously to Bemis Heights to get more reinforcements from Gates.

Burgoyne realized the same thing Benedict did. He was in serious trouble. He was forced to call on his third river column to send reinforcements. They would have to abandon their supply lines along the river. Burgoyne knew that if Benedict led one more thrust at him, he would be finished.

When Benedict reached headquarters, he was breathless and eager to request more men to finish off Burgoyne. Gates resisted, still wringing his hands and indecisive. He had already told Benedict, that morning, not to expect reinforcement. Intimidated by a very agitated

Benedict, Gates consented to release a small division.

Benedict, not wanting to lose the momentum of the battle, ran to his horse and was heard shouting, "By God, I will soon put an end to it!" Gates could not stand the thought of Burgoyne surrendering his sword to the likes of Benedict Arnold. Gates sent out an express rider with orders for Benedict to return to headquarters.

With the delay caused by Gates, Burgoyne had time to get his third column ready to reinforce his lines. He made a quick surge into the American force. Without Benedict and with darkness falling, the Americans retreated back to Bemis Heights.

If only Gates had quickly reinforced Benedict, or if he even made his own move on the British river column, Burgoyne would have been finished that very day. The British army had paid a high price, with 556 killed, wounded or missing. Patriot losses were more modest—63 killed, 210 wounded and 38 missing.

Burgoyne regrouped his men and began digging entrenchments and setting up redoubts on the north side of Freeman's Farm. Not knowing what the next American move would be, the British hastily buried some of the dead in shallow graves and gathered their wounded. Some wrote: "That in the middle of the night, large groups of wolves could be heard feasting and howling over the carnage."

There were many accolades written about the American performance on September 19th of 1777. One of the most telling was written by a British officer who reported: "The courage and obstinacy with which the Americans fought were the astonishment of everyone. They had shown they were not the contemptible enemy we had hither to imagined them, incapable of standing a regular engagement."

But the battle was not over. Burgoyne still had a considerable force, although somewhat crippled and its supplies almost totally cut off. He could dig in and wait for possible reinforcements, inflicting major damage to American forces, or he also could possibly try to punch through American lines on his way to Albany.

Burgoyne's army was now like a wounded beast, at just a mile from Bemis Heights. The next real phase of the battle would be behind the American lines. Gates and Benedict were about to lock horns.

Benedict implored Gates to attack the British the next morning, before Burgoyne could erect any strong defenses. He knew that many brave American soldiers would have to spill their blood to try and breach the entrenchments. Gates and his adjutants completely ignored Benedict's pleas and he had to fight to keep his composure. Day after day, Gates sat in headquarters, refusing to make any strikes on the weakened British army.

Gates' favorite adjutant, James Wilkinson, who he affectionately called "Wilkie," wrote of the September 19th events to Congress, saying he wasn't even sure General Arnold was in the field, giving all the credit of any action to the "Brave General Gates." He also belittled Daniel Morgan's actions.

Of course, Gates and Wilkie didn't know who was in the battlefield that day. The only knowledge they had of September 19th was the sounds of the battle from a mile away. Gates was feeling very threatened by and jealous of Benedict's growing reputation among the troops.

One officer wrote about Benedict: "He alone is due the honor of our late victory. He has earned the life and soul of the troops, enjoying the confidence and affection of his officers and soldiers. They would, to a person, follow him to conquest or death." Another officer wrote: "Arnold was not only the hero of the field on September 19th, but he had won the admiration of the whole army."

Benedict endured insults from Gates and his faithful adjutants in his headquarters. Benedict was feeling that his honor was threatened. He was becoming furious at being ignored.

The whole matter peaked on the night of September 22nd of 1777. Benedict charged into Gates' small headquarters and a shouting match broke out. One officer wrote of the generals that they were using "high words and gross language."

Gates relieved Benedict of the command of his wing. Before he left, Benedict demanded a general pass, to go to Washington's division to "Possibly have it in my power to serve my country." Benedict stormed back to his tent to try and calm down. Now, the clash between the generals was out of headquarters and out in the open.

The officers, on hearing of the confrontation, began to panic and they tried to reconcile the men—but to no avail. The field officers held a separate meeting and composed a letter: "From General officers and Colonels," thanking Benedict for his service and conduct, but "requesting him to stay in camp."

A groundswell of support from his men caused Benedict to relent and he said that he would at least stay in camp. He was completely dejected, very angry and determined to formulate his own plan of action.

Gates became upset by the lack of support from the men and officers, but continued to ignore Benedict. He threatened to arrest him for insubordination if he tried to take command. Granny Gates sat on his hands for almost two weeks, hoping Burgoyne and Benedict would just go away.

During a war council, Burgoyne's officers suggested retreating to Canada. Gentleman Johnny "wouldn't hear of it." He simply couldn't accept the humiliation he would receive if he left a numerous army in the field with the ability to travel south to attack General Howe in New York City. Burgoyne's supplies were running dangerously low and he decided to advance, again, toward the American army's left wing. He sent a large reconnaissance force along the ridgeline toward Bemis Heights.

Even after hearing reports of enemy movement, Gates continued to be unresponsive. Daniel Morgan decided he would take the initiative. With the help of two other divisions, he encircled the British reconnaissance force and drove them back to Freeman's Farm.

Around three o'clock in the afternoon, Benedict heard the roar of cannon and musket fire, from his camp. He knew Burgoyne was making a move. Benedict had decided he was prepared to die for his men and his country. He strapped on his sword, put his pistols in their holsters and rode his horse madly toward the engagement.

On that brightly colored fall afternoon, Benedict appeared from nowhere in the field at Freeman's Farm, under no orders but his own. Some wrote: "He had a fierce look of determination on his face."

Benedict first encountered a unit from his old home state of Connecticut. He asked the men, "Whose regiment is this?" They responded, "Colonel Latimore's, sir." Benedict shouted to the men, "God bless you, boys. If the day is long enough, we'll have them all in Hell before night."

A rousing shout of huzzahs went up as Benedict entered the field on his powerful, brown horse. He quickly located Latimore, who gladly granted Benedict's request to take command. Benedict rode back and forth in front of his troops with his sword drawn, quickly aligning forces to make a charge.

The British, seeing the general they had to face before, and hearing the roar of huzzahs across the field, knew they were about to be in a fight for their very lives.

Benedict spun his horse to the left toward Daniel Morgan's riflemen, who were engaged in a fierce firefight with General Fraser's light infantry. He could see Fraser on a gray horse, riding behind his lines and giving instructions. Benedict shouted to Morgan to have his sharpshooters cut Fraser down. Daniel Morgan understood Benedict's thinking, even above the echo of musket fire.

Morgan sent his best sharpshooter, Timothy Murphy, up a tree to take out Fraser. On his third attempt, Murphy's musket ball hit his mark.

The British lines panicked on seeing their commander

fall from his gray horse and quickly retreated toward Freeman's Farm. In the mass confusion of Fraser's retreating column, Burgoyne directed fire to cover the retreating troops.

Benedict quickly seized the opportunity and led a massive charge into the other British flank. Some later wrote of Benedict's actions as he rode between the warring armies, that he must have gone mad or was drunk with too much rum. Men had never seen a commanding general charging in front of his troops.

Spurring his mount on, Benedict rode between the two armies as they fired intensely at each other. As the British cannons blasted grapeshot, many American soldiers fell during the charge. Whatever the men were facing, Benedict was impressive and inspiring.

Astride his horse, Benedict was so close to the British lines that his view from horseback gave him the advantage of being able to peer over the British entrenchments. He realized the charge was aimed directly at the strongest part of the British defensive fortifications. He quickly turned his horse to the left, looking for a weak spot in the British defenses.

With lead flying at him from all directions, he spotted a weakness between the major British redoubts—about 120 yards wide—that was lightly defended. Benedict shouted to his men to follow him and pointed his sword toward the weak spot in the enemy lines. He then spurred his horse and charged through the British lines himself, with his men pouring in behind him.

In the heat of battle, Benedict was slashing his sword wildly at the enemy. He even accidentally wounded the head of an American soldier, which he apologized for later. He said that because of the intensity of the fight, he wasn't aware it had happened.

Now, the Americans held the fleeing, panicked British troops in a deadly crossfire. But one retreating regiment of Hessian soldiers quickly reformed a line and fired a volley of musket fire. All aimed directly at Benedict. One musket ball shattered the bones in Benedict's left leg. The others hit his horse. The animal reared into the air and fell directly onto Benedict's wounded leg, pinning him to the ground as it thrashed till death. From his position beneath the horse, Benedict commanded his men to "pursue."

In an act of revenge for the shooting of his general, one young American soldier was ready to bayonet a wounded Hessian. From under his horse, Benedict called him off. He said to the young man, "He was only doing his duty."

As the men poured through, they were able to extricate Benedict from under his bold, but lifeless mount. Colonel Henry Dearborn asked Benedict if he was badly wounded. Benedict replied, "In the same leg" and he "wished the ball passed his heart." Shortly after, he passed out from the pain.

Darkness fell on the battlefield as what was left of the fleeing British army retreated for the cover of trees along the Hudson River. Benedict had his complete victory, but at a high price. However, Benedict would have said that many others paid even more.

Benedict was loaded onto a makeshift stretcher and then a medical cart, enduring a slow, bumpy ride to an army medical hospital set up in Albany. Soldiers along the way thanked and encouraged him as he tried to focus, despite the pain.

Burgoyne formally surrendered his sword to Horatio Gates, somewhere near the village of Saratoga on October 17th of 1777. Gates, who never once left headquarters or showed himself anywhere near the battlefield, audaciously ignored Benedict and proclaimed himself "Hero of Saratoga."

Benedict's only consolation was that the officers and men in the struggle knew the truth of the battle, and even Burgoyne himself credited only General Benedict Arnold for his defeat.

CHAPTER TWENTY

A Long & Painful Winter for Arnold & America

While Benedict was fighting Burgoyne, George Washington had his hands full. General Howe made a move against the American army at Brandywine Creek. Both sides suffered heavy losses and Washington was driven back.

By late September, British forces under Howe occupied the Capital at Philadelphia. Congress relocated the capital first to Lancaster, Pennsylvania and then to York, Pennsylvania. The only good news of the campaign season was the defeat of Burgoyne's army. As Washington retreated across the Pennsylvania hills, he ordered Gates to send reinforcements. But Gates was slow to react, perhaps wanting Washington to stumble.

For his victory at Saratoga, Gates had a medal in his honor struck by Congress. He then designed a vicious political campaign to elevate himself, to the point of trying to replace Washington. Benedict's long recovery gave him no chance to defend his actions, or relay the truth about General Gates.

Over the next five months, Benedict was flat on his back, trying to recover, while enduring horrible pain. The surgeons wanted desperately to amputate his leg, but Benedict wouldn't allow it. They put his leg into a device called a traction box, wired down so the leg couldn't move. Benedict felt like a wounded, caged animal, trapped in his own body. His leg had to be re-opened to remove bone splinters. That leg atrophied terribly and became a full two inches shorter than the other leg.

Benedict survived the ordeal, but would be crippled and in pain for the rest of his life. However, he wasn't the kind of man to be kept down. He had a special shoe with a two-inch lift made for him, and he was determined to ride and walk again, someday.

As he had lain in a prone position for so long, he continuously asked for information on how the war effort was going. Many of his officers and troops visited him regularly, which lifted his heart. It also gave him much time to think.

Benedict believed strongly about the "cause" of liberty. He dreamed of a new country where men were created

General Horatio Gates. He betrayed Arnold at Saratoga and attempted to betray Washington. *Courtesy, Library of Congress.*

equal. Those were high words, but he sometimes became bitter, seeing how rank, privilege, bloodlines and wealth trumped the actions and efforts of so many. He also thought about how the members of Congress had written of sacrificing their lives, property and sacred honor. But it seemed to him, he was one of the few willing to put deeds and actions above words.

As he looked death in the face, Benedict's business was nearly broken and many stepped harshly on his honor. If he recovered, he was determined to set some things straight.

One of Benedict's more distinguished visitors during his recovery was the Marquis de Lafayette. Lafayette had arrived from France, seeking adventure and glory in the fight for American freedom. He attached himself to George Washington. He had heard of this fighting General Arnold and wanted to meet him. Lafayette heard from Benedict and other officers truthful accounts of how the Battle of Saratoga really went down.

But the Marquis was an aristocrat's aristocrat. On returning to Congress, he still gave credit for Burgoyne's defeat to Horatio Gates, since he was the ranking general in the field and higher in status than Benedict. Lafayette's betrayal, actions and manner just fueled the fire within Benedict. He did not trust the French and really hoped they wouldn't be any part of the new America.

He had watched men bleed and die for the cause of liberty and the end of British tyranny. Why would they want to align themselves with another monarchy? Especially one where the elite and privileged used men like pawns for the cause of furthering themselves. When Benedict heard of Lafayette's alliance with Gates, he knew he was right not to trust the French. He had lost faith in many of the elites in Congress. Even his "Excellency," George Washington, was acting at times more the part of a king and not a general.

Benedict had gone into action quite naïve, but now he knew merit and actions weren't always enough. There were those who, without honor, would elevate themselves. It was a very long and painful winter for Benedict, but by spring, he was very slowly regaining his health.

Washington was in a desperate situation at Valley Forge. He surely needed the assistance of men like Benedict, who could get things done. He wrote to Benedict of "an earnest wish to have your services in the ensuing campaign" and promised "A command which I trust will be agreeable to yourself and of great advantage to the public."

Benedict could not take the hospital life any longer. He hired a cart to take him home for a while, so he could see his boys and his sister, Hannah. On the way there— on March 12th of 1778—he penned a letter back to

General Marquis de Lafayette, who betrayed Arnold after Saratoga.
Courtesy, iStockphoto.

Washington. His journey home was delayed by a couple of weeks, as the rough ride in the cart caused his leg to re-open. More bone splinters had to be removed.

His attending surgeon said the cleansing process "will be a work of time" and take perhaps two to six months. Benedict informed Washington that it was with "utmost regret" that he could not form "any judgment," regarding when he might "repair to headquarters" and "take the command your Excellency has been so good as to reserve for me."

Benedict finally made it back to his home in New Haven and got some rest, although he was still in horrible pain from his wounds and surgeries performed to remove bone splinters from his leg. It did his heart good to spend time with his family. But Benedict's sense of duty wouldn't let him rest for very long.

The fallen General Arnold knew his country was at a pivotal moment. The British were occupying Philadelphia. Washington was backed up to the hills of Pennsylvania at Valley Forge and preparations for the following year's campaign were sure to begin soon. Benedict then planned to travel to Valley Forge by carriage since he couldn't ride yet. Not even a shattered leg would prevent him from fulfilling his sense of duty to his country.

On May 6th of 1778, Washington received news that France had entered into alliance with the now-recognized United States. Washington was ecstatic and he proclaimed "A day of rejoicing throughout the whole army." He ordered 13 rounds of cannon fire and loud huzzahs for the king of France and the American states. With Lafayette at his side, he then reviewed his troops.

Washington must have wondered how Benedict would receive the news. The next day, in an appeasing way, he wrote to Benedict: "That he had received a gift of epaulets and sword knots that he reserved for Benedict, when he arrived." He knew the alliance was mostly a result of the American army's actions at Saratoga, during the defeat of Burgoyne. He also knew that Benedict was no fan of the French and hoped his fighting general would be placated by the generous gift.

By May, morale at Valley Forge was horribly low. Baron von Stueben had been helping the situation by performing troop training and discipline. But the cold, wet conditions, lack of food, supplies and clothing made for a very angry and quiet camp.

Washington did not expect to hear from Benedict for months. As he sat in his cozy headquarters at Valley Forge, with his servants and Lafayette, suddenly the camp erupted in loud huzzahs. Men were cheering wildly. On investigation, Washington discovered that Benedict had arrived by surprise, in a carriage, on May 21st of 1778.

The men were joyful. Their fighting general was back! Washington must have been more than a little jealous that he could not raise that kind of support from his men. Lafayette was also quite bewildered. He had never seen so much adoration for a common officer.

As Benedict settled into camp, Washington presented him with the gift of epaulets and sword knots. They began going over plans for the upcoming campaign season.

In May, British General Howe, because of his poor showing the previous year, was replaced by British

General Henry Clinton. Clinton, fearing a blockade of French ships, withdrew his troops from Philadelphia and sent them back to New York City.

Americans began reoccupying the Capital by mid-June. Washington decided, since Benedict was still recovering from his wounds, that Benedict should take command of defenses in Philadelphia, at least until he was in condition to take the field.

Washington also had an ulterior motive. This assignment would separate Benedict from his adoring troops. He knew that the cesspool of backbiting politics in the capital would probably ensure Benedict was no threat to his own command. Lafayette also thought the politics of Congress would probably eat alive a lower class general like Benedict.

Lafayette and Washington were getting a bit paranoid. George had just barely survived an attempt by Horatio Gates to replace him as commander-in-chief. Word was spreading, especially among the troops, who had really won the Battle of Saratoga.

George was beginning to see Benedict as a possible threat to his power. But he had trust in Benedict, since he knew Benedict didn't really have any political aspirations, as men like Gates had. Nonetheless, he would keep an eye on Benedict, since no one could muster troop support like he had.

CHAPTER TWENTY-ONE

Capital Commander & Introduction to Politics 1778

By June of 1778, Benedict assumed command of the nation's capital city. Washington attempted an attack on the returning British army, which resulted in the Battle of Monmouth, in New Jersey. The two-day fight was pretty much a standoff, as one of Washington's generals ordered a retreat against his orders. Clinton's forces marched back to New York City.

Congress returned to Philadelphia by July of 1778. George Washington set up headquarters at West Point, New York. From West Point, Washington continued monitoring Clinton's actions through an extensive spy ring he created and maintained to watch Clinton's movements and other interests he had throughout the colonies. The spy ring was extremely secretive and would later be known as the "Culper" spy ring. It could be said it was the forerunner of today's CIA.

Also in July, France declared war against Great Britain and sent a fleet of ships to attempt a combined siege of British forces in Rhode Island. The whole effort failed because of slow American troop movements and bad weather for the French fleet. The French were forced to move their ships to Boston for repairs.

As Benedict took command of the situation in Philadelphia, he learned about all the worst elements of capital politics. A group of Republican-minded state officials confronted Benedict with demands of how he should handle citizens suspected of collaboration with the British during the long occupation. They insisted on severe punishments that included hanging.

Benedict refused to comply with their demands. He recognized the citizens were only trying to survive the occupation and he wanted reconciliation. This action by Benedict infuriated many bloodthirsty, zealous patriots and they accused Benedict of high-handedness and of having the emblems of a military dictator.

Most of Benedict's worst political enemies were active in the "Constitutionalist Party." They were quick to slander anyone they suspected of having Loyalist tendencies, branding them "Tories."

Since Benedict insisted on maintaining order, they began a smear campaign against him. By February, Benedict's adversaries had declared eight alleged abuses of power, which were all trumped-up charges that they had no proof of.

Benedict, as he had in the field, took the offensive. His honor meant everything to him and he would not have his good name slandered by anyone. He demanded that Congress conduct a court of inquiry to examine his actions. The Constitutionalist Party asked for a delay, as they said they needed time to collect evidence.

Going on the offensive with Congress, Benedict became the first advocate for veteran's rights. He badgered Congress with his memories of men bleeding and dying in service to their country, while Congress had made no provisions for their widows and children. Benedict formed a fund raising campaign for some of them, contributing a substantial sum from his own accounts. His compassion shamed Congress into taking an interest, and they made some effort to provide assistance for fallen veterans and their families, at least in the case of officers.

Benedict grew so weary of the politics that he wrote in one letter: "I daily discover so much baseness and ingratitude among mankind that I almost blush to be of the same species."

As fall and winter dragged on, Benedict finally got his requested court of inquiry, in an attempt to clear his name. The court found him guilty of two of the eight counts against him, charging that he had abused military authority. The claim was that he allowed a merchant ship, that he had invested in, to leave port when others could not and that he used government wagons to move cargo to the ship. The court recommended he be turned over to Washington for a reprimand.

The court could find very little he had done that was less than honorable. Benedict was incensed. He was considered a mere provincial by the elites in Congress.

By May, Benedict had reached his limit when it came to petty politics and he wanted Washington to get on with his proceedings so he could be in the field again. He wrote to Washington in frustration: "I want no favor. I ask only for justice, having made every sacrifice of fortune, blood and become a cripple in the service of my country. I little expected to meet the ungrateful returns I have received from my countrymen. But as Congress has stamped ingratitude as the current coin, I must take it."

Benedict felt betrayed by an elite and French-loving Congress, but expected Washington to insist his name be cleared of all charges. However, Washington reprimanded him and let the charges stand.

That act disparaged Benedict. He was betrayed by Gates at Saratoga and now he wondered if Washington was also setting him up for betrayal.

History books would explain these political events and portray Benedict as a dark and angry person. But reality was quite different. Benedict was always ready to defend his honor, but was also a champion for the common people and wanted what was best for his country. The hot political atmosphere of colonial Philadelphia would be a test for anyone, especially if the job was to maintain civility and order in the city, along with defending it.

As commander, Benedict attended many social events that winter, where he met and courted Margaret "Peggy" Shippen, the daughter of a wealthy neutralist. Benedict fell madly in love with her. She was described as intelligent, vivacious and very beautiful. She was attracted to this energetic and handsome general. Surely, his courtship throughout the winter and into spring of 1779, kept Benedict in quite high spirits. He proposed to Peggy and they were wed on April 8th of 1779.

CHAPTER TWENTY-TWO

1779:
The American Revolution is in Serious Trouble

In early 1779, the British launched a ruthless military campaign through the southern states. They immediately captured Savannah, Georgia, and a month later, Augusta. By May of 1779, the Brits had burned down Portsmouth and Norfolk, Virginia.

Washington was still busy trying to analyze Clinton's plans for the force entrenched in New York City. In June, Clinton made a move up the Hudson River, keeping Washington either pinned down or in retreat. Loyalists and Indians had been raiding and massacring settlers in central New York.

The American army defeated the Loyalists and Indian bands in Elmira, New York and launched a retaliatory campaign against the tribes responsible for massacres of settlers. Some 40 Indian villages were burned down throughout the Finger Lakes region.

John André, head of British Intelligence and friend of Mrs. Arnold.
André helped Benedict escape. He was later hanged by Washington.
Courtesy, iStockphoto.

Benedict maintained his post in Philadelphia and, to Washington's surprise, managed to survive quite well politically.

Congress was busy trying to negotiate a peace plan with Great Britain and there was even talk of reconciliation. But the rebels held strong, insisting on independence and complete British evacuation.

Congress was not always the noble group of forefathers future generations were led to believe.

Abigail Adams wrote to her husband, John, saying that Congress should appropriate funds for an orphanage in Philadelphia to care for all of the illegitimate children Congress was going to leave there.

By late September, John Adams was appointed by Congress to negotiate peace with England. In October, Washington set up his winter headquarters in Morristown, New Jersey. That very spring and summer, it has been reported that Arnold began corresponding with British Major John Andre.

John Andre was described as handsome, artistic and highly educated. He was a true romantic. He loved painting, poetry and played the flute. He was fluent in English, French, German and Italian. It was said he enlisted in the British army to mend a broken heart after a long courtship was ended.

Andre was sent for two years of special training in Germany. By 1774, he had obtained the rank of lieutenant and was shipped off to Canada. He became involved in the American army's siege of St. Johns and he was taken prisoner. Andre was transferred to Lancaster, Pennsylvania. As an officer, he was allowed to stay with a local family, instead of in a prisoners' barracks.

Andre was moved into the home of the Caleb Cope family, where his ability to speak German fluently served him well. He gave art lessons to the family's oldest son and became a close friend of the family. At the end of 1776, he was put on a prisoner exchange list and sent to General Howe in New York City.

While in New York, Andre presented to General Howe a memoir he wrote about "observations in the colonies." Howe was quite impressed and made him an aide to Major General Charles Grey.

Grey was an adversary associated with Washington in the Battle of Brandywine Creek and the Battle of Monmouth. But he was also part of the invasion force that led to the occupation of Philadelphia. During the long occupation, Andre attended events where he wrote poetry for the "Ladies of Philadelphia." One of those ladies was Margaret "Peggy" Shippen, Benedict's future wife.

Peggy, being from a neutralist family, was quite smitten by this dashing young officer and he with her. Andre may have even considered courtship, but times as they were, would not allow it. Nevertheless, they remained very good friends.

The long-held belief that Benedict corresponded with Andre about treason and switching loyalties had some serious flaws. The letters produced as evidence were not in Benedict's handwriting and may have even been fabricated.

It is possible that Benedict, fearing the downfall of independence and worries for his new wife, children and sister in Connecticut, may have entertained an outlet in case the situation for the colonies went badly. That stance was possibly encouraged by Peggy.

That Benedict or Peggy could have even contacted Andre at that time seems highly improbable. But is possible Andre may have found a way to contact them, as he wanted to keep in contact with Peggy. With Benedict's famous fighting style, he may have thought that Peggy might soon become an available widow and he cared deeply for her.

As Clinton succeeded Howe in New York, Andre was promoted to a major in November of 1778 and appointed to Clinton's staff. Clinton, seeing his varied resourcefulness, made Andre head of British intelligence. That appointment may have gained his access to Philadelphia.

But another likely scenario is that Washington's spy ring may have known Andre's position as head of intelligence and was keeping an eye on his activities. The Culper Spy Ring may have reported Andre's friendship with Peggy to Washington and he may have kept this information as future ammunition, in case Benedict became too popular.

In the winter of 1779, Washington stayed encamped in Morristown, New Jersey and spent yet another winter of supply shortages and very low morale among the troops. He experienced many desertions and faced mutiny attempts.

In late December, Clinton made a surprise move and set sail from New York City with 8,000 men. He headed for Charleston, South Carolina, arriving there on February 1st. By early April, Clinton attacked the defenses at Charleston. Washington sent reinforcements, but it was too little, too late.

By May 6th of 1780, the British captured Charleston and by May 12th of 1780, the Americans suffered the worst defeat of the war. Charleston was the home of the entire southern army of about 5,400 men. Clinton also captured four ships and the entire military arsenal. The defeat reflected quite poorly on Congress and the commander-in-chief.

What was worse is that on May 25th, as Washington was still in Morristown, he faced a very serious attempt at mutiny, by his own men. Two continental regiments conducted an armed march through the camp and demanded payment of salary that was five months overdue, along with full rations. They knew Washington wasn't going hungry.

A number of Pennsylvania troops helped put down the mutiny. Washington, trying desperately to maintain discipline, ordered that the two leaders of the revolt be hanged. Hanging his own men didn't endear Washington to his troops.

By June of 1780, Washington was in serious trouble. Congress had lost confidence in his abilities. They needed a general who could win some battles and drive the British from the south. Benedict had the proven ability to accomplish the task, but Congress considered him a mere provincial.

Congress called on their pet general, Horatio Gates, to head the southern command. Benedict knew Gates lacked any offensive strategies and didn't have the courage or ability to take on the British. He would later be proved correct.

Just ten days later, on June 13th, the British tried another offensive move in New Jersey, hoping to draw out and take on a decisive battle with Washington. But they were met by forces under the command of General Nathanael Greene. Greene's brother, Christopher, had fought with Benedict and was part of the Kennebec march through Maine.

The British managed to loot and burn most of the town of Springfield, but were thoroughly beaten by Greene's forces. Finally, America had another victory. It would be the last time Britain would make a push in New Jersey.

On July 11th of 1780, the French arrived at Newport, Rhode Island with 6,000 soldiers under the command of Count de Rochambeau. They would remain in that area for nearly a year, blockaded by the British fleet.

CHAPTER TWENTY-THREE

A Tale of Intrigue Far Different

Most prominent historians write about the next months of General Arnold's life, using terms like "We'll never know why" or "only by Divine providence." But they seem to always look back at the conclusions made before any evidence was presented. If the evidence is viewed critically, it is questionable and far different from what most believe.

In the winter of 1779, Benedict and Peggy found out they were going to have their first child, a baby boy born on May 19th of 1780.

By August of 1780, Benedict was more than eager to get back on the battlefield, having quite enough of Philadelphia and Congress. Later, he penned words regarding the civilians in Congress, "They could not admire or reward the virtue they cannot imitate."

Benedict's wounded leg was getting stronger and he was wondering what duties Washington would require of him. The obvious best placement for him would be in the southern theater with his old friend, Daniel Morgan. But with Gates in command, that was ruled out, at least at that time. Benedict would have no part of serving with or under Horatio Gates again.

Supposedly, Washington offered Benedict command of his left wing and Benedict declined in favor of the West Point command. This would have truly been out of character for a warrior like Benedict. It seems the only post offered to him was command of West Point. The appointment made Benedict suspicious of Washington's thinking and intentions.

It has also been widely reported that Benedict kept himself busy by weakening the defenses around West Point, but the evidence shows just the opposite. In fact, just two weeks prior to the alleged treason, Benedict wrote to Washington, informing him that he had found some unserviceable cannons at the fort. They weren't battle ready, but they could be used as warning beacons on the Hudson River, in case of an enemy advance.

Benedict had a warning post constructed, to alarm the fort in case of enemy attack. That action would have been quite strange behavior for someone who was accused of betraying the fort's defenses.

Two weeks into Benedict's new command, Horatio Gates, who Congress sent forth to the southern command, finally showed his true colors. Gates gathered his forces in Hillsborough, North Carolina and marched south toward Camden, South Carolina. He thought he would easily rout the British forces there. Unfortunately, he ran into a sizable column of British regulars under the command of British General Lord Cornwallis. Against the wishes of his officers, Gates decided to engage the British in battle.

The decision proved disastrous for the southern army. A bloody battle ensued, causing 750 casualties and close to 1,000 men were captured by the British. Before the battle was over, Gates and his aides rode hard north, supposedly seeking assistance. By nightfall, Gates was a good 60 miles north of the battlefield. He was accused of cowardice in the face of the enemy. A very embarrassed Congress asked Washington to appoint a new southern commander.

Surely, when Benedict received the news of Gates' performance in South Carolina, he must have felt quite vindicated. He probably expected to be called up by Washington and asked to take the southern command. Benedict certainly would have been the obvious choice. Daniel Morgan, his fighting ally, was already in the theater and Benedict had the proven battle experience to get the job done.

But Washington also knew that if he sent Benedict south and he found a way to defeat Cornwallis, Benedict would be the obvious choice to replace Washington and be the hero of the whole country. Washington had other plans for Benedict.

Throughout the late summer of 1780, Benedict had written contact with Andre, mainly since he was a trusted friend of his wife, Peggy. To placate her, Benedict entertained the idea of joining the British. He didn't like the French alliance and he no longer fully trusted Washington. If Washington betrayed him, where else could he turn?

The whole idea of betraying his country, after he had given so much, seemed quite ridiculous. After all, Benedict had in-laws in Philadelphia, a new wife and baby soon to arrive at West Point, as well as three sons and a sister in Connecticut—the site of his home and business. Unless he was forced into a desperate situation, it is hard to believe that he had any serious intentions of switching allegiances.

Benedict wanted to see what Washington's intentions would be for his appointment. He was anxious to either join the fight against Cornwallis in the south, or be included in efforts to strike Clinton in New York City. But unknown to Benedict, some of his communications with Andre had been intercepted by the

Culper Spy Ring, then under the leadership of Major Benjamin Tallmadge.

Tallmadge was the equivalent of the head of today's CIA and he reported only to Washington. He had spies in the hundreds under his command. Tallmadge reported to Washington about the friendship between Benedict's wife and Andre. He told Washington that Benedict had asked Andre what the terms would be if he did switch sides.

By late summer, Washington was feeling intense pressure from all sides. Congress was losing confidence, the war effort was stalled or going badly, mutiny by his own men was a growing threat and the French had some major concerns.

Washington was setting up a meeting with Count Rochambeau in Connecticut. The French needed reassurance that when this fight was over, "His Excellency," George Washington, would ascend to the throne or the Presidency. The French were willing to get involved in this fight with Britain, but they had put all their eggs in one basket.

Behind Washington, the French needed to know no rivals would take his place. When Horatio Gates failed miserably in the south, it only left one hero in the way of Washington's sole ascension to power.

Benedict was a very popular, wounded warrior. He had been the only truly victorious general in the war effort. He also had the full trust, support and admiration of the officers and the troops—which Washington, at that point, did not.

The French also knew that Benedict didn't value the French alliance. Benedict's feeling, which he wasn't afraid to make public, was that if true patriots fought hard enough, they could run this country and win the war without allegiance to anyone.

Lafayette and the alliance counseled Washington that he should find a way to discredit Benedict or get rid of him before he became the people's choice. Washington wanted to reassure Rochambeau at their meeting in Connecticut that the Benedict problem would be dealt with.

Washington and Tallmadge began plotting a way to push Benedict into going over to the British. Through the Culper Spy Ring, they had enough evidence to accuse him of treason. But Washington didn't want to just accuse Benedict of enemy collaboration, nor did he want to put him on trial and give him a platform to defend himself for talking to the British.

Benedict's popularity would make Washington appear petty and it would just look like slander and jealousy of someone who had sacrificed so much for the cause of liberty. Washington also knew honor meant everything to Benedict, and that in a public forum, he could easily defend himself, since his actions were so far above reproach.

Tallmadge and Washington thought they could use Andre's weakness for women and his affection for Peggy, and the truth, as their greatest weapons. Tallmadge had a female agent known only as "The Lady 355." He directed her to befriend Andre. She may even have been having an affair with Andre. This could have been the avenue for the interception of correspondence between Benedict and Andre.

Tallmadge's lady spy was instructed by him to go ahead and tell Andre that she was part of the Culper Spy Ring and that she had sensitive information that Washington knew about Benedict's correspondence with Andre. She was to say that Washington intended to use the information for the arrest of Benedict, so he could be charged with treason and collaboration with the enemy.

Andre's softness and adoration for Peggy spurred him to make solid accommodations for Benedict if he would switch alliance to the British crown. Andre couldn't bear the thought of Peggy or her husband being disgraced and dragged through the mud by Washington.

Tallmadge and Washington decided to spring their trap in the last week of September 1780. Tallmadge instructed his agent, Lady 355, to inform Andre that

Washington was meeting with the French, and planned on arresting Benedict for treason in late September.

When Benedict took command of West Point in August 1780, he set up his headquarters across the river from West Point—and a little south—at the home of a Loyalist, Colonel Beverley Robinson, who was serving the British. The "Robinson House" was a grand home. The Robinsons were actually friends of Washington before the war broke out.

Benedict thought it would be a good command position and he hoped to send for Peggy and their baby to join him at his new post. Peggy arrived from Philadelphia and embraced Benedict for a happy reunion on September 14th of 1780.

Andre sent word to Benedict that they needed to have an urgent face-to-face meeting. Benedict enlisted the help he needed to set up the meeting. He asked for help from a very distrusted and questionable man named Joshua Hett Smith. He was known to play both sides in the war and some said he was maybe a double or even triple agent.

Helping people communicate with each other, on both sides of the war, was a lucrative business for Smith. Joshua Smith offered Benedict the use of his home for the meeting and means of transport for Major Andre, who was going under the code name, John Anderson.

Smith's home was just south of West Point, on the same side of the river, not far from a ferry crossing at Stony Point. Unknown to Benedict, Joshua Hett Smith was also working for Tallmadge and Washington.

Though communications were dangerous and difficult, Benedict managed to get in contact with Andre—going under the code name John Anderson—who was aboard the warship, Vulture, anchored in Haverstraw Bay, near Dobbs Ferry and Smith's home. They arranged a private meeting for the night of Wednesday, September 20th.

Smith had taken his family to Fishkill, New York, north of the Robinson House, to visit family there and empty his home for the secret meeting between Benedict and Anderson, also known as Andre. Joshua Hett Smith arrived back at Robinson House midday on the 20th to tell Benedict all preparations were in place for the secret meeting.

Benedict wrote passes for Smith and two servants—brothers Joseph and Samuel Cahoon—and a John Anderson (Andre) to cross and recross near Kings Ferry at all times. Benedict also supplied a boat to be available for Smith. The very same day, Washington was meeting with French General Rochambeau.

Smith claimed he couldn't find Benedict's transport or round up the Cahoon brothers to row in time to make the meeting. He sent one of the Cahoon brothers back to Robinson House late that night to inform Benedict. All night, Andre waited for a rowboat that never appeared. That situation gave Smith time to inform Tallmadge's agents about the meeting. Smith was specifically instructed that, in no way, was Andre, "Anderson," to get back on that boat when the meeting took place.

Tallmadge or his agents wanted Smith to escort Andre overland, back to British lines—with exact routes—and to make sure "Anderson" was in civilian clothes. They would take care of the rest.

The next morning, an angry Benedict rode to Kings Ferry to take charge of what went wrong with his meeting. There was a note from Andre waiting for him at the ferry. The note said that despite the missed connections, they could still meet that night.

Benedict crossed the river and rode to Smith's house to confront Smith and the Cahoons. The boat he had arranged for was in plain sight, and surely, he was nervous about the possibility of foul play. He stayed in the area that day to make sure the night's rendezvous went as planned and to keep an eye on Smith.

By late evening, Benedict sent Smith and the Cahoon brothers by rowboat to pick up Andre, who was aboard The Vulture. Benedict waited on shore with an extra horse, to take Andre to Smith's house for the meeting. Andre boarded the small craft in uniform, with a cloak to cover the bright, red color of his uniform.

Andre and Benedict finally met face to face at about 2 o'clock in the morning. Benedict informed Andre that they could ride to Smith's house, but Andre said it wasn't necessary, as what he had to say wouldn't take too long, and then he could be rowed back safely to the ship. For the next two hours, the men had much to discuss.

Very possibly, Andre related to Benedict the information he received from Lady 355, that Washington—pressed by the French—intended to have him arrested for treason. Andre had made arrangements with Clinton for Benedict to be received as a British general on the British side. Benedict couldn't believe what he was hearing, but knew Washington was acting strangely, and he wasn't sure he could still trust him.

Benedict thought, at first, maybe it was a ploy to capture him. But Andre was more than sincere and a good friend of Peggy. He also, to reassure Clinton that Benedict was sincere, needed some information about West Point. They may have drawn a crude map of the point with numbers of soldiers at redoubts, or this information might have been planted on Andre later.

But the West Point information Andre had on him at capture was not anything of much consequence. Clinton insisted he must have details about West

Point, to prove Benedict's intentions to serve Britain were honorable.

It doesn't appear likely that Benedict had any intentions of surrendering his many friends at West Point. But if Washington intended to arrest and betray him, there was no way he could continue to serve his country. He thought Washington was coming to West Point to offer him the southern command, but Andre said he would only offer him a trial, where he could try to defend his honor, or be sentenced to the noose.

For Peggy's sake, Benedict should take the generous offer from Britain. Benedict's mind was racing. What if Andre's information was wrong or—even if it was correct—could he still defend his honor at trial? He knew, at least, that his actions over those many years had been above reproach.

By four o'clock that morning, Benedict and Andre had discussed all they needed to. Benedict still wasn't sure what action he would take, but thanked Andre for his concern for him and Peggy. Smith approached, saying the hour was too late to row back to The Vulture and the Cahoon brothers were too tired to make the journey. They had left for home, with the transport.

Alarm bells should have gone off in Andre's and Benedict's heads at that moment, but their minds were still racing and both were dog tired. They decided that rather than argue with Smith, they would ride to Smith's home and wait until the following night to row Andre back.

As Andre and Benedict continued their discussions at Smith's house that morning, cannon fire erupted from the eastern shore of the Hudson. The shots were aimed at The Vulture. The ship returned fire, but had to retreat farther south. Benedict should have been proud of his men. He had, just weeks prior, encouraged that type of decisive action against any British ship that tried to get too close to the Point.

But it would make Andre's return trip much longer. Andre wasn't really stranded; it was simply a little longer row down river.

Smith insisted, with this shelling, that more eyes would be on the river, so he and Mr. Anderson should go overland back to the British line. He would accompany Mr. Anderson, otherwise known as Andre, safely on horseback. Benedict needed to get back to his post, as he knew Washington was due there soon and he had to make a final decision on what course to take.

Andre felt calmed. He had done all he could for Benedict and his friend, Peggy. Benedict wrote passes for Smith and Anderson to return to British lines by land or water, and made his ride back to Robinson House.

Smith insisted that Mr. Anderson change into civilian clothes. Alarm bells should have gone off in Andre's head at that point. Also, he could have rowed himself back if need be, but he went along with Smith's insistence on an overland return route. Smith took him on an indirect route north through patriot lines, across the northern ferry point, using Benedict's passes. Witnesses remarked that Smith was especially chatty with all the travelers they met, as if he wanted to leave them with a lasting impression.

The two men made their way south on the eastern side of the river, until dark. Then, they took shelter at a house along the way, sharing a single bed that the residents offered to travelers. Early the next morning, they continued south. About 15 miles from the British lines, at a place called Pine Ridge, Smith pulled up his horse and told Mr. Anderson he should be safe to ride the rest of the way on his own.

The area between the two armies was a no man's land. Smith told Anderson to take a right at the next fork in the road, wishing him a safe journey and left him there. Tallmadge's plan began to go wrong at that point. Had Andre taken the right fork in the road, as instructed by Smith, he would have gone directly into Tallmadge's hands. But Andre, suspicious of Smith and his odd actions, decided to go left at the fork in the road.

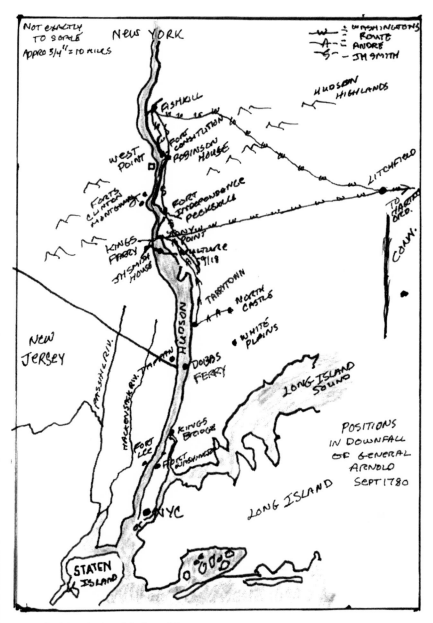

Positions in Arnold's downfall.

As Andre rode on, three men pulled him over at gunpoint. In this land of chance, there were many gangs loosely affiliated with either side. Some reports identified them as militia, others as simply highwaymen trying to rob Andre.

But the word was out that the Americans were looking for a Mr. Anderson. The three men searched Andre and found some papers that they probably didn't understand, since only one of them could read. Andre offered them money if they let him go and showed his pass from Benedict. They likely laughed, since they already had his money. If they let him go, they surely wouldn't see him again.

Thinking they may be rewarded, Andre's captors decided to take him to the nearest American post in North Castle, headed by Colonel John Jameson. Knowing that there were standing orders to be on the lookout for a John Anderson, Jameson told the three men that if there were any reward, he would contact them.

Jameson looked over the situation, papers and the pass found on Andre. Apparently, after reviewing the paperwork, he didn't see any treason at West Point and decided to send Mr. Anderson to General Arnold for questioning.

By that time, Tallmadge was frantic. Andre never showed at the right fork of the road, as expected, so he began backtracking to find out what went wrong with his capture plans. He found out that three men were taking a prisoner to North Castle. When Tallmadge arrived at North Castle, he began to fix the situation and take control. He ordered an express rider to overtake the guard escorting Anderson to Benedict and to bring Anderson back to a secure site in South Salem, for questioning.

Historians would now have us believe Jameson, in the confusion, decided to notify Benedict of Andre's capture and detention. But for some unknown reason, Jameson decided to split the evidence and send the paperwork to General Washington. That whole part of the story has no credibility, whatsoever.

If Colonel Jameson couldn't find enough information in Anderson to suspect treason and sent him to Benedict for questioning, why wouldn't he send the evidence with the prisoner, for Benedict to sort out? And, if he suspected treason or spying or any involvement by Benedict, he wouldn't have sent Anderson to Benedict.

The next series of events appear to have been very carefully orchestrated by Tallmadge and Washington. Tallmadge had a rider sent to Benedict, informing him of Mr. Anderson's (Andre's) capture and that the information about the capture and papers regarding defenses at West Point were sent on to Washington. This was intended to push Benedict over the edge and force him to flee rather than face trial for treason by Washington.

Another rider was sent to Washington with the damning information, maybe with some added to it, along with a confession by Andre.

Tallmadge, at South Salem, took personal charge of Andre. He took Andre's confession and told him he might as well sign it. His fate was sealed anyway, as a British officer behind enemy lines in civilian clothes. Tallmadge probably told Andre if he ever mentioned George Washington, he couldn't guarantee the safety of Peggy Arnold.

While all of this intrigue was going on, Washington had wrapped up his meeting with the French and was supposed to be en route back to West Point. But supposedly for security reasons, he didn't take a direct route back to West Point the same way he came. He veered north and spent the night, first in Fishkill, New York. There, he met with none other than Joshua Hett Smith.

Many historians like to leave this encounter out of history books. Perhaps Smith told Washington he did exactly as instructed. He got Andre, dressed in civilian clothes, to the capture point for Tallmadge. It will never be known what Smith told Washington or how he was compensated, but Washington also assured Smith that if a trial ensued, he would be found innocent of any part of a treason attempt.

Washington assumed Andre was safely in Tallmadge's hands and that Tallmadge would be sending riders out to Benedict to see if he would leave West Point and another rider to him with the evidence he needed, but the rider had not reached him yet.

On the morning of September 25th of 1780, Washington needed to buy some time for all the plans to fall into place. He took his time and sent his slave ahead to Robinson House to tell Benedict he was coming for breakfast. As Washington, Lafayette and Washington's entourage of about 40 men rode toward Robinson House for breakfast, Washington made an odd move.

Noted in the writings of some members of the entourage, George wheeled his horse off the path to inspect fortifications down by the river. Some of his men complained that surely Mrs. Arnold would be getting the breakfast ready. They asked why George didn't do his inspection after breakfast. He told some of them that they could ride on, but that he intended to make his inspection. From that vantage point, he may have used his spyglass to see if he could spot Benedict rowing down the river.

That morning at Robinson House, Benedict was waiting for the arrival of General Washington. He was hoping this would be a happy day and that he would be asked to take the southern command. But Andre's warnings of arrest put him on edge. Surely, he would defend his honor at trial, if Andre's information were correct.

The breakfast hour was getting late. At nearly 10 a.m. there was still no Washington. The junior officers of Washington's entourage arrived and asked if they could join Benedict for breakfast. He had already eaten, but he warmly greeted them and seated them for breakfast. Then appeared another officer, Lieutenant Solomon Allen.

Allen had just ridden in with an express letter from Colonel Jameson, who was on the east side of the Hudson River. Benedict invited the lieutenant to sit down and have some breakfast. This was completely normal behavior for Benedict. His men were always welcome in his company and they respected and admired him for it.

As the men talked, Benedict sifted through the dispatch Allen had just delivered. The dispatch stated that a Mr. Anderson was captured, with his pass and concealed documents that were sent on to General Washington. Benedict seemed visibly shaken. He ordered his horse be saddled and he went upstairs to talk to Peggy. Andre was right. Washington, himself, was betraying him. Benedict told Peggy he would have no country left to serve in.

Benedict told Peggy he would try to send for her, but he must escape and take the British outlet Andre had arranged, or stay and try to defend his honor against a stacked court. Peggy wanted her general alive and told him he might better serve England, than be betrayed by his own countrymen. He mounted his horse and rode to the docks by the Hudson. He gathered a crew of men and had them row hard south down the main channel in the river, toward enemy lines and the warship, Vulture.

Washington, from his vantage point north of Robinson House, might have watched Benedict row south or he may have been just buying time for Tallmadge's rider to reach Benedict.

Either way, Washington was hoping Benedict would take the bait. He made a good show of inquiring about Benedict's whereabouts until the second express rider arrived with the paperwork he needed. Washington knew he had his bases covered. If Benedict didn't defect on his own—as he hoped—he would still have the evidence to accuse him and put him on trial.

As Washington's aide brought him the news of "Arnold's Treason," one of his entourage wrote of the unusual calm in Washington's manner. On hearing noise from upstairs in the Robinson House, Washington confronted Peggy Arnold. Shaking and crying, Peggy clutched her baby in fear for her life. Another aide wrote that it was the only time in the war when he saw Washington break down and weep.

Washington's aides thought it was the news of Benedict's treason that shook him so deeply. But at that moment, Washington's heart must have been heavy, knowing that to further himself and to satisfy the French, he had just sold America's greatest patriot, literally, down the river, destroying his life and family in the process.

Once Washington composed himself, he had to attend to the cleanup operations. He began a feverish letter writing campaign to inform everyone he could about Benedict's horrible treason.

Andre also needed to be taken care of. Tallmadge had personal care of Andre until his trial a few days later. Tallmadge surely reminded Andre that if he mentioned Washington, his friend, Peggy, would pay the price. Andre played the gentlemen to his death. At trial, he was found guilty. Normal procedures were that British officers were valuable trading tools in prison exchanges.

But Tallmadge and Washington couldn't risk having Andre talk. Washington sentenced Andre to death. Andre requested he at least be shot as a gentleman, but Washington stuck to strict protocol, insisting that since Andre was captured in civilian clothes, he must die by hanging.

The only other person besides Tallmadge and Washington who knew the whole plot was the agent, Lady 355. After Andre's hanging, she disappeared, with no one knowing her fate. What she knew could not be revealed and war can be a dirty business. We can only guess what happened to her.

Joshua Hett Smith didn't really know the whole story, but was put on trial for his role in the treason events. Somehow, possibly with the help of Washington, Smith was found to be an innocent player in the matter. Because Andre didn't go from Smith directly into Tallmadge's hands, Washington was worried about what Andre told the three highwaymen who captured him.

Washington personally looked for the three men and bestowed on them lifetime pensions, farms in New York and the first medals awarded any soldiers in the United States. He paid them quite royally for their loyalty and silence.

Aboard The Vulture, Benedict wrote to Washington to plead for Peggy's life, saying she had nothing to do with his actions. He accepted his fate and took the commission in the British army, set up for him by Andre. He hoped to no avail that being on the other side would inspire others to switch their allegiance and help him retake his country.

Washington spared Benedict's family, owing him that at least. But the smear campaign that branded him a horrible traitor was far-reaching and effective.

Later, under orders from Clinton, Benedict fought for the British in Connecticut and tried to interrupt supply lines in Virginia. But he never fought with the ferocity he had as an American general. He was pretty much just doing his job. His heart was no longer in the fight.

While Benedict was in Virginia, Washington issued an order to Lafayette that speaks to the truth of this tale. He ordered that if Benedict were captured or engaged, he must be killed. Washington didn't want a captured Benedict telling his story.

Washington's best move after the demise of Benedict was that he appointed Nathanael Greene as commander of the southern army. Greene, with the help of Daniel Morgan and others, finally managed to back Cornwallis up to Yorktown.

Surviving yet another mutiny attempt, Washington switched his efforts—with the help of the French— from New York City to Yorktown, Virginia. He had to hurry, but managed to get there as Cornwallis was under siege and the French fleet was blockading any British escape. Of course, Washington accepted all the credit for defeating Cornwallis and the great victory there, propelling him to the coronation of the American presidency he had so long been seeking.

Benedict moved his growing family to London and eventually tried to revive his trading business in New Brunswick, Canada. He went nearly broke, lending money to settlers in Canada who couldn't pay him back, never showing any signs of the greedy traitor he was portrayed as.

Peggy and Benedict had four more children, and finally, in trading ventures in the West Indies and Canada, they managed to pay off all creditors. Benedict continued to sail and command ships, despite his crippled leg. He left many trading partners, friends and some family in Canada. He had one illegitimate son in Canada, probably with a woman between his wives. Benedict provided for that child in his will.

Benedict remained a man who fiercely defended his honor. Even as he moved to London, Benedict called out an individual who tried to brand him as a traitor for a duel.

Peggy was a very devoted wife and mother. She always had high praise for Benedict and she always referred to him as "her general." Benedict's sons went on to serve with honor in the British military.

Benedict Arnold died in 1801 at the age of 60, and is buried in London. If this author were to ever visit there, an American flag would thankfully be placed at his grave. If it weren't for the valiant efforts of men like Arnold, America would have never won her independence.

Whether the theory presented in this book is upheld as plausible, or torn down by historians, Benedict Arnold surely deserves respect for all he gave for this country.

CHAPTER TWENTY-FOUR

The Evidence

Historians would have us believe that General Arnold went from the captain of his own militia group in 1774 to a major general in the American army. He fought countless battles, endured crippling war wounds, fought and shared suffering with his friends, gave up all he held dear—his home, business and time with his family—all for the "cause" of liberty. He became the hero of nearly the whole country.

Then, historians say, he became disenchanted of his own accord—and in less than five months—decided to betray his country.

The evidence shows many odd events and questions still surrounding the events of 1780. The Culper Spy Ring set up by Washington wasn't even discovered until a century after the course of events related to Arnold unfolded. Many historians still refuse to take a critical look at the people involved, but I feel from what I have learned—after all these years—questions still remain and deserve further recognition.

First of all, we are told Arnold began correspondence with the British in May of 1779, one month after his marriage to Peggy Shippen. The letters I've seen to date are not in Arnold's handwriting, and who knows, may have been fabricated, possibly by the Culper Spy Ring.

Also, the contents of the letters give little information of any consequence. Just considering the logistics of setting up secure communications with the enemy, in 1779, makes any correspondence highly questionable and improbable.

We have always been told that General Arnold weakened the defenses at West Point. But every indication I've seen shows just the opposite. In fact, he installed warning posts just ten days prior to his alleged charge of treason.

I have not seen any evidence that Arnold was offered any post other than West Point, with the exception of Washington's word for it. I feel that after Washington gave Arnold a reprimand and assigned him to West Point, he may have been very suspicious of Washington's intentions toward him.

Historians would also have us believe Joshua Hett Smith was a simple, unwitting go-between who Arnold used for logistics. Smith's actions in September of 1780 are very suspect.

First of all, Smith bought himself a whole day by claiming he couldn't round up the Cahoon brothers or find a boat on the Hudson River. By sending one of the Cahoon brothers to inform Arnold the meeting was off, instead of going himself, gave Smith ample time to inform Tallmadge or others of the meeting taking place.

The next odd thing about Smith's behavior was that, on completion of the rendezvous, he couldn't get the help available to row Andre back to board The Vulture, forcing Andre and Arnold to go to Smith's house. On top of that, insisting to go overland to British lines was safer than simply rowing the following night down river—a very short distance. Even if the ship were farther down river, it would still have been the safer route to row by water rather than going overland through a war zone.

Smith then insisted Andre, aka Mr. Anderson, change into civilian clothes, which led to Andre's death. That strange behavior continued as witnesses recorded his "chatty" behavior and the drop off of Andre, directing him to the right fork in the road, which would have taken him directly toward American lines.

Many historians also leave out the fact that after dropping off Andre, Smith had a meeting with Washington in Fishkill, before Washington made his journey to West Point.

It seems quite clear Smith was working both sides in the treason accusations. It's bizarre that Smith, at a subsequent trial, was found to be innocent of anything to do with treason.

An interesting side note is that the next year, county officials jailed J.H. Smith for suspected Tory sympathies, and he escaped in woman's clothing to New York City before going to London during the British evacuation of New York City.

Also related through history, is that Andre was captured by accident, with papers found concealed in his boot. But I wondered if evidence was added later, since Colonel Jameson, the first commanding officer to review the situation, decided to send Andre to Arnold for questioning. Apparently, he didn't recognize treason in what Andre had in his possession.

Suspect also is that Andre would end up directly in the hands of Washington's head of intelligence, Major Tallmadge, and remain under his supervision until he met his end. It seems far too coincidental that Andre would just happen to meet up with Washington's CIA chief and be kept personally under his guard.

Also, some of the alleged papers in Andre's possession were reports from officers other than Arnold, making me wonder if some of Andre's papers were planted on him.

The next bizarre event in this tale is the sending of express riders to both Arnold and Washington. The warning of both men never made sense. If you suspected Arnold of treason, you wouldn't send a rider to warn him and tell him you sent the paperwork to Washington. And, if you thought otherwise, why wasn't the pass from Arnold—held in the possession of Andre—respected?

I think the rider sent to Arnold, telling him of the capture of Andre and the papers sent to George Washington, was meant to push him over the edge and cause him to flee.

The next hole in the treason story is Washington's trip to Fishkill for the night. The easier and most direct route to West Point would have been farther south, directly to Robinson House. We are told George went north through the hills for security reasons, but he had made the journey safely and without incident just a few days prior. Also rarely mentioned is Washington's meeting with Joshua Smith at Fishkill.

The tale gets even harder to swallow when, on the next morning, Washington—supposedly en route to Robinson House—sends his servant ahead to tell Benedict he's on his way for breakfast, and then makes his way to the river instead. There's a very good chance that Washington watched Arnold row down river or was stalling for time.

Also, no one ever mentions the strange sight of a whale-boat with American soldiers aboard, rowing hard toward enemy lines.

It was a common practice, throughout the whole war, that when an enemy officer was captured, that person would be used as a very valuable trading tool for prisoner exchange.

But Washington saw to it that Andre was hanged, even though many spoke out in his behalf. Washington would not relent, refusing Andre's request to at least be shot as a gentleman. Apparently, Andre didn't feel his actions were spy material.

Through research, there seems to be no evidence of any imminent attack planned for West Point by the British. A British assault on the point would have also put Arnold's wife and baby in harm's way.

I also feel it is quite odd that General Washington, who had seen and heard of countless acts of heroism on the battlefield during his years of war, bestowed the first medals ever awarded to soldiers to three men who were probably just trying to rob Major Andre. On top of that, they were richly awarded farms and lifetime pensions.

Chilling also was Washington's order to Lafayette that if Arnold were captured or engaged, he must be killed. For some reason, he needed to have Arnold silenced forever.

I feel only five people knew the whole story: Washington, Tallmadge, Lafayette, Andre and Lady 355. It's quite interesting that after the treason event, she simply disappeared and was never heard from again.

Through years of study, I have concluded that Arnold switching sides of his own accord would be completely out of character. Arnold was a man whose honor meant everything to him. On the numerous times his honor was questioned, he became defensive to the point of calling for the drawing of pistols.

It surely wasn't about money. Arnold—to a fault—was generous throughout the war, with almost everyone he came in contact with. He constantly used his own funds to continue the war effort.

Time and time again, for the sake of his country, Arnold charged headlong into cannon and musket fire. He fought for America like no warrior had ever fought, with no regard for his own safety. He never sent a soldier on a mission that he wouldn't do himself. It won him the respect and admiration of his troops, an accomplishment that no leader of the times could claim.

Although Congress treated him quite shabbily because of his class status, Arnold still held his own politically, earning the respect and loyalty of men like Ben Franklin, John Adams and Philip Schuyler.

For Arnold to sell out West Point, he would also have to consider his holdings in Connecticut—his house and his business—his sister, his three sons, his in-laws in Philadelphia, not to mention his new wife and baby.

If Washington really wanted Arnold to return to stand trial, he surely could have gotten word to Arnold and reminded him of that, as he held all of the cards. I think Washington just wanted Arnold to go away, and he made it easy for him to do that.

Washington and his French allies had the motive to rid themselves of a potential problem, given Arnold's hero status. They couldn't let a mere provincial colonist gain the heart and soul of the army, and possibly rise to the rank of leadership in the new country.

All events of September 1780 point to a set up of epic proportions. I don't believe Benedict Arnold betrayed his country, but that he was betrayed by his country.

I feel that the possibility of Arnold switching sides in a war that he had given so much for is truly remote and absurd. I believe a way was devised to crush "The Dark Eagle."

This book is dedicated to General Benedict Arnold, with grateful thanks for what he did for my country. We would not have won our independence without him.

CPSIA information can be obtained at www.ICGtesting.com
Printed in the USA
BVOW030525291012

304178BV00001B/2/P